YESTERMAN: Journey of Fate

YESTERMAN

Journey of Fate

Carl J. Lapeyrouse & Christopher A. Gayle

Created by Carl J. Lapeyrouse

BALANCED Media | Technology

McKinney, Tx

Published in the United States by

BALANCED Media | Technology

McKinney, TX 75069

Publisher's Note: This is a work of fiction. Names, characters, businesses, places, events, and incidents are either the product of

Yesterman: Journey of Fate / Lapeyrouse & Gayle. – 1st ed.

ISBN (paperback) 978-0-9963966-2-2

ISBN (ebook) 978-1-7327438-1-6

Dedications

*To my beautiful wife, Michelle, and my two
beautiful children, Livi and Jack. I love you all so
very much.*

*To my mother, Rita Lapeyrouse, who always
believed in me and in my ability to manifest my
dreams. How apropos as the basis of this story
came to me in a dream. I love you Momzo!*

*Finally, to my writing partner and best friend,
Chris Gayle, who helps convert my creative ideas
to reality.*

Carl

*To my love, my refuge, my solace, my wife —
my Julie.*

Chris

Image Credits

Yesterman Logo by Patrick Bertinelli
Cover Design by A. Fred Matamoros

PROLOGUE

The couple emerged from the Chicago Public Library and bounded down the damp stone steps, swinging their five-year-old son by the arms between them. The cold moist air of the dreary day was biting. The sky couldn't decide if it wanted to rain or snow, so it settled upon a dense fog that enveloped the family like a cold wet blanket. They didn't mind though; they were happy. They had spent all afternoon at the Express-Ways Children's Museum, which occupied two hallways of the library. They were excited for the opportunity to visit. The young couple had found it challenging of late to keep their son engaged and stimulated. He was so bright, so inquisitive. They read to him consistently and listened as he read to them. They played every genre of music for him and took him to symphonies and plays. They expanded his mind with board games and puzzles. He seemed to absorb everything as if he were a sponge newly dipped into water. Clearly their child excelled. They knew that he was destined to be exceptional.

Today's excursion was their first foray to the children's museum, and the child was enthralled by the experience. He had spent hours manipulating the exhibits and questioned his parents incessantly about them. They had not yet made it to their car and he was already asking when he could come back. His father helped him into his booster seat, which was situated in the back of the family's blue four-door 1980 Plymouth Volaré, stretched the lap belt across him and latched it securely.

"We'll come back next weekend," promised his father as he buckled his son into the booster seat.

Assured that his son was secure, he closed the child's door, and then closed the door to the front passenger side into which his beautiful wife had settled. He tapped on the child's window as he made his way around the back of the car, and was acknowledged with a smile. As he situated himself into the driver's seat and fastened his seatbelt, his wife turned to her son.

"I love you, baby," she said.

The little boy now smiled at his mother. "I love you more, mommy," he said in his child's voice.

He did not know that he would forever treasure those last words he and his mother shared. For at that moment his father turned the key in the ignition switch of the car, and the little boy's world was torn asunder by a massive explosion. Shrapnel tore into his legs his heavily padded coat fortunately protecting his torso. Blood and flesh splattered his torso and face. His mother and father disappeared before his eyes in a burst of flames. He screamed for them, but he could not hear his own voice; the ringing in his ears was deafening. Fire poured from the engine compartment into the front of the car; the cabin filled with toxic black smoke and the smell of burning hair and vinyl. Tongues of fire rushed along the floor of the car and the little boy felt the heat scorch his feet as his tennis shoes melted onto them. Instinctively he moved to free himself from the booster seat. He struggled with the seatbelt latch but finally managed to disengage it.

Once free of his constraint, he rolled out of the seat and maneuvered to the opposite back car door. The door would not open, the heat having expanded the metal. He depressed the button in an effort to lower the side window but the mechanism would not function. He pounded on the window in an attempt to break it but to no effect. He was too small to generate the force needed. He began gasping for air as the fire consumed the oxygen inside the car. His eyes and lungs stung with the acridity of the smoke and fumes. He pressed his face and hands to the window, pleading for someone to let him out as he attempted to see through the smoke and fog.

"Please," he whimpered.

Exhausted and depleted of air, his little body crumpled into the seat against the rear door. Suddenly, in his waning consciousness the little boy heard a crash of glass as the back window shattered, raining fragments upon him. Flames rushed over his head with a roar and jetted out of the rear breach. Two strong black-gloved hands penetrated the inferno, grabbed the little boy by his collar and waistband, and pulled him through that same opening into the cold moist air as his world went dark.

2

Jack Dawson was a beast of a man. Standing six-foot three-inches and weighing 190 pounds, he was a handsome, modestly chiseled, lean, fit, physical machine. He had a rugged, yet professional appearance. His hair was wavy and thick, but well-trimmed. His eyes were soulful and penetrating. Jack was out for an evening jog. He ran the hills of San Francisco with the same ease that most people ran on a treadmill at a slight decline. Jack had always excelled athletically. From grade school through college he was a varsity starter in every sport in which he participated.

But there was more to Jack Dawson than just brawn. Yes, he was handsome and physically adept, but his greatest asset was his intellect. In graduate school he finished first in the Harvard MBA program and now, in his mid-thirties, he was the youngest Senior Vice President in charge of domestic trading at Hughes Investments, one of the most prestigious investment banking firms in the country. He'd received that promotion just over a year ago. Jack was driven; he was driven in every aspect of his life. Every day he ran at least five miles, to wind down and clear his mind at the end of his workday.

That was exactly what he was doing when he found himself yet again in his old neighborhood of Russian Hill, passing in front of his old home. And yet again he began to reminisce about his life in that house with his beloved wife, who was now nearly six months dead. For Jack, the grief had not waned. Six months was no magic number; the loneliness was just as profound now as it had ever been. Jack slowed his pace as he passed the house, which he could not bring himself to sell. He imagined his wife working in the front flowerbed as she had so often done. She loved adorning her yard with seasonal flowers, he remembered fondly. For a moment he thought that he actually saw her. Jack choked down the lump in his throat and guided himself back to where he now lived at the edge of the historic district of San Francisco.

Jack had moved to the warehouse loft apartment three months ago. He needed an escape from the heartache that his Russian Hill home had become. The memories there were too painfully sweet and intense. He had hoped that the nightmares would stop with the move. They had not, but at least they were not recurring nightly. Jack rented his loft apartment from Steve Oberman, who lived and worked in the downstairs of the old two-story brick warehouse. Steve was a reclusive forty-something-year-old whom Jack noted to be anxious and hyper vigilant. Jack presumed this was because their domicile was not in the trendy gentrified part of the historic district, but rather in a more seedy section. Hearing an occasional gunshot was not uncommon. But Jack wasn't discriminating when he had searched out the place. He was desperate for a move, and this location was available and close to the financial district where he worked. As Jack ran up to the old building he saw Steve wrestling a large, apparently heavy box out of the back of his Subaru Forester.

"Hey Steve, can I give you a hand?" Jack asked.

Steve returned his greeting with a furtive glance and a dismissive shake of his head as he dragged the box toward the warehouse.

"No, I got it," replied Steve.

Jack shrugged and picked up a newspaper that was lying at the foot of the metal stairway that once served as a fire escape for the second floor of the warehouse. He gave Steve a wave of acknowledgement and made his way up to his apartment.

That is one weird dude! thought Jack.

Jack unlocked the metal door at the top of the stairs and made his way inside. His apartment was rather rustic. The original worn, wide-planked pine floors covered its entirety. Exposed iron beams and posts supported a tin roof; brick walls made up the perimeter of the room. The kitchen was functional and the apartment was decorated in a Nuevo eclectic design, courtesy of his sister. It wasn't really his taste in furnishing, but again he didn't really care. He would have been happy with the air mattress and hard-backed chair that had been the only furnishings present when he took out the lease. His apartment was meticulously ordered, reflective of what he wanted his life to be. The apartment over time had become comfortable for Jack, and it was conveniently located.

Jack kicked off his shoes upon entering, made his way to the fridge for a bottle of water, and headed for the shower. Clean and refreshed, he made himself a meal of leftover sushi and a desiccated liver with wheat germ shake. He sat on the sofa with his meal and watched Fox Business News before heading off to bed at 10:00 p.m.

As was his custom at night, Jack went to his closet to pull out his clothes for the next day. Just like his apartment, his closet was well ordered: suits on one side aligned by color, casual clothes on the other. The only thing that appeared out of place was a stack of boxes on the floor of the closet, all labeled "Holly." Jack opened a box on top and pulled out a sweater, pressing it to his face and nose, trying to breathe in her scent. Though Holly's fragrance had long ago faded from her clothes, Jack was determined not to let the memory of her smell and feel and face fade. After a moment, he returned the sweater to the box, pulled out his black Armani suit and hung it upon his valet. Jack settled himself into bed, set his radio alarm for 6:45 a.m., and lay down to sleep.

The night passed fitfully with yet another series of disturbing dreams. It was time for such a night, as Jack had had two nights in a row of relatively peaceful sleep. When NPR's *Morning Edition* began to play on KQED, he was already awake, remembering the nightmare that was his dream and his wife's death. He wiped the sweat from his brow and forced himself out of bed and into the shower.

Jack made himself ready for the day, donning his black Armani suit. As had become his habit over the past few months, Jack sat on his sofa sipping a cup of coffee, and read his morning devotional. Since Holly's death, he had become more attuned with his spirituality. It had always been so important to Holly and now he wished he had shared that with her when she was alive.

Morning time seemed to be the hardest for Jack. He tore himself away from his readings and memories and descended the stairs to his car parked below. Jack drove the black 740 IL BMW to work, pulled into the garage, and maneuvered into his reserved parking space. It was curious to him, the things that just no longer seemed important. He had always been so driven. He strived for success and he had enjoyed the perks that success offered. As he walked into the building, he mused how he would have done so much differently, had he known what was to befall his wife. He was proud of what he had accomplished, but he regretted all the time he was away from Holly. *Why was I in such a hurry?* he wondered.

Jack's day started like any other as he greeted the firm's receptionist as usual.

"Good morning, Marion."

"Good morning, Mr. Dawson. At it early again today I see," Marion observed

"Early bird gets the worm, right?" he said. Jack walked by her with a smile and a wink. He entered the elevator, where he was joined by a very attractive brunette.

"Good morning," he said, casually acknowledging her.

"Hey there; how are you this morning?" she inquired as she turned to face the doors.

"Couldn't be better!" he lied.

They rode together in silence until the elevator stopped at the tenth floor. As Jack slid by the girl to exit the elevator at his floor, she sneezed. A rather stifled sneeze at that, Jack noted.

"Bless you," he said as the door closed behind him, and made his way through the complex to his private suite of offices.

"Hey Jack, coffee and doughnuts in the break room," said a co-worker passing by.

"Thanks, Bill."

Jack entered his office suite where his secretary Betty, a matronly lady in her early sixties, was sitting at her desk.

"Good morning, Mr. Dawson," she said.

"Good morning, Betty," Jack replied.

"Gary Jacobs is looking for you. Shall I get him on the phone?" Betty asked.

"Sure, that would be great. He's at it early this morning," said Jack with a smile as he entered his personal office. He closed the door behind him and sat at his desk.

Gary Jacobs was a partner in the firm and Jack's immediate supervisor. He had taken on the role of Jack's mentor when senior partner August Hanson passed away two years ago. Hanson was the one who recruited Jack for the firm while Jack was still in graduate school. He had had some connection to Jack's father, that is his adoptive father, which Jack never fully understood. From day one, Hanson had taken Jack and Holly under his wing. Jack credited that attention for his success and rapid rise in the firm. Hanson, however, always thought that Jack was trying to progress in the firm too rapidly. He had frequently admonished Jack to slow down and spend more time with his beautiful wife. But Jack remained determined to excel. Hanson had always dreamed of making Hughes Investments an international financial powerhouse. He had told Jack that when the time was right, they would work on that dream together. Hanson never got the chance, so upon his death Jack took over that nascent project and developed it into a comprehensive plan, which he had presented just last week to the partners. Jack remembered the old man fondly and had of late regretted not taking his sage advice.

Thinking of Hanson brought Jack back into his

reverie of Holly and feeling that he would do so much differently, if only he could. He was jolted back to reality when Gary Jacobs entered the office. Gary was a slight man of alabaster complexion and sandy white hair who was fifteen years Jack's senior. His booming voice was quite discordant from his physical appearance.

"Hey sport!" Gary roared. "Don't get too comfortable. You need to pack up your stuff and get out of here."

Jack was quite perplexed. "Get out of here?" he asked. "Is something wrong? Was there a problem with the Hanson report?"

Gary laughed. "A problem? Heck no...the partners loved it!" he said. "You're going on vacation for two weeks so we can get your office ready!"

Jack was even more confused. "What's wrong with my office?"

Gary sat down across from Jack. "You're moving upstairs," he said. "You have been named as the head of the newly formed Hanson International Investment Division. You've been made a partner, Jack."

Jack was dumbfounded, speechless. Gary continued:

"I'm proud of you," he said. "August would be proud too. And I know Holly would be as well. Congratulations, Jack. Now pack up and get out of here. We'll see you on the fifteenth floor two weeks from today."

Gary stood as did Jack, and shook his hand. As Gary left, Betty walked in carrying a cup of coffee and wearing a smile. "Congratulations, partner," she said. "I'd best get packing; we've got a big move to make!"

Jack was elated as he pulled out of the office parking garage. He had called his mom and dad from his office to tell them the news. His dad had been out of the country and his mom had flown to New York to meet him upon his return. They planned to stay the week in New York City. Jack was just about to call his sister Emily when the phone rang. Seeing that it was she, he answered in hands-free mode.

"Hey Em!" he said.

The excited voice of his sister resounded through the car's speakers. "Jack, I just got off the phone with mom! When were you going to tell me?" Emily asked.

Jack attempted to respond. "I was actu…"

He was interrupted as Emily pressed on. "That is *so* cool!" she said. "So are you moving to Europe? Oh I hope you move to Spain! I *so* want to go to Spain. Are you moving to Spain, Jack?"

"Well Em, it's not…"

"When do you start?"

"I'll start in two…"

"I bet you're getting a *huge* raise!" Emily broke in.

"Em…"

"You know what? You're going to take me to dinner!" she announced.

"Emily!" Jack shouted over his sister's voice.

"What?" Emily said, finally catching a breath.

"I'm not moving," said Jack. "I'm staying right here in San Francisco, at least for the time being. But once this division takes off, who knows where I might end up. As for your other question, I start in two weeks. They've given me a vacation so they can get my new office suite ready. You'll have to help me decorate! And, I've already planned to take you to dinner at Farallon. I've made reservations for tomorrow night at eight. Are you free?"

"Ooooo! Farallon! You *did* get a raise," she said. "Of course I'm free. When was the last time I had a date?" Emily laughed at herself. "Hey, since you're off for the next bit you can hang out with me! How 'bout we hike Muir Woods tomorrow? We haven't done that since…" She stopped abruptly.

Jack completed her thought. "It's okay, Em," he assured her. "We haven't done that since we went with Holly… I don't know, I think I'm just going to stay in until dinner. I'm not quite up to that yet."

"Look, I know you're still having a hard time, but don't you think that maybe it's time to get back out there? Get back into your life? You can't hide in your work forever, Jack."

Jack knew that his sister was trying to be helpful but he couldn't suppress his annoyance with her. "We've talked about this before, Emily," he said. "Let me decide when I'm ready."

Emily relented, seeing that she had hit a sore spot. "Okay, but one of these days I'm going to kidnap you and make you get out," she said.

Jack softened. He knew that his sister had good intentions. "We'll see about that. I'll pick you up around 7:30 tomorrow evening, okay?" he asked.

"That sounds good. I'll see you then. Bye now, and congratulations," said Emily.

With that Emily disconnected the call and Jack turned up the music, remembering that last hike that he had under the sequoias with Holly. It had been a beautiful fall day. Emily and her man of the week were with them. Jack remembered that Holly was telling him he was working too hard. She wasn't being pushy, but he knew that she wanted and needed more of his time. Walking hand in hand under the canopy of the trees, he promised her that he would spend less time with work and more time with her. He meant it, too. He remembered her leaning her head against his shoulder. He recalled just how happy he was at that moment. The remembrance was short lived, as within five minutes he had arrived at his destination. Jack pulled his car into the lot of his favorite Asian market. He decided that he was going to start his vacation with a liver shake and sushi. As he entered the grocery he was greeted by the now familiar clerk.

"Hello, Jack. What can I get for you today?"

Cho was a gorgeous twenty-year-old college student of Asian descent who worked at her parents' market in the afternoon and evening hours. She was a fireball with purple punk hair, a nose ring and a dragon sleeve tattoo down her left arm. Jack could tell that she was very bright. He liked her.

"Hey Cho, let me have some desiccated calf liver,

wheat germ and two California rolls please. I'm just going to pick up a few other things."

"Sure, take your time," she said.

Cho scooped the desiccated liver and wheat germ into separate containers. She wrinkled her nose at the liver as she did so. "Hey, how do you eat this stuff?" she called out to Jack. "It smells awful."

Jack laughed as he headed down the aisle. *It* was *awful,* he thought.

He picked up a few essentials and headed back up to the counter. He grabbed a newspaper from the rack and placed it with his purchases upon the checkout counter. As Cho packed up his meal, Jack glanced down at the newspaper. It was the second byline that caught his eye:

Slaying in Park. Police have no leads

The article stated that the body of an unidentified young woman was found in Golden Gate Park by early morning joggers. She was apparently the victim of a late night mugging. Cho noted the newspaper article as she rung up Jack's bill.

"It's terrible what happened to that girl," she said. "This place is getting crazy."

"More so every day," Jack replied as he paid. "Have a good night Cho. Be safe," Jack said as he folded the paper and gathered up his groceries.

Cho smiled a goodbye. "Thanks, Jack. See you next time," she said.

As Jack backed out his car, he made casual note of a white utility van rounding the corner and pulling into the parking lot of the market. His attention though was on the rancid smell of desiccated liver wafting throughout his car. Jack pulled out onto the street and headed home. For the first time in a long time, he felt at ease. But he wished Holly were at home to enjoy this feeling with him.

3

Before Jack settled down to his desiccated liver and wheat germ shake and California rolls, he went for his evening run. He had told himself that he was not going to go by his old house today; he was going to try to do as Emily suggested and move forward with his life. But he did run by his old home. The memories were painful, but it was all that he had left of Holly. He clearly was not ready to let go and move on.

Jack negotiated the hills of San Francisco with ease. He cleared his mind when he ran, and he prayed. He was comforted by his conversations with the Lord. He was coming to know what a special relationship that was, a relationship that Holly knew so well and had yearned to share with Jack. He kept on running. Though he didn't feel fatigued, he noted that dusk was upon him. He headed back home, not wanting to run through his own neighborhood after dark.

As he approached his home, he once again caught sight of Steve unloading cargo. Not out of his Subaru this time, but rather off of a flatbed trailer. And this time he had help. Two men that Jack surmised to be about the same age as he had just heaved a tarp-covered pallet off the trailer and were moving it toward the warehouse. Jack approached the group and once again offered to help. And once again Steve declined his offer, much to the dismay of his two assistants.

"Okay, if you're sure," said Jack.

"Thank you, but we can handle it," said Steve.

Jack bounded up the metal staircase and retrieved the key that was tied to the drawstring of his shorts. Just as on every other night of late, Jack showered, enjoyed his meal and dressed for bed. He made ready to pull out his suit, and chuckled when he remembered that he didn't have to go to work the next day. So instead, he settled on the sofa and turned to the local news while sifting through his mail. *Maybe I'll watch a movie tonight* he thought, knowing that he could sleep in tomorrow. His heart sank when he heard the reporter utter the following:

"In breaking news, San Francisco Police report that Cho Nguyen, the clerk and daughter of the owners of a local market, was killed this afternoon during the course of what appears to be a botched robbery."

Jack looked at the television screen. Megan Hart, a mid-twenties auburn-haired broadcast journalist, had the look of the girl next door but the reputation of a tenacious bulldog in the field of investigative reporting.

"Ms. Nguyen was found dead on the scene, the victim of a single gunshot wound to the head. A police spokesman stated that Nguyen activated an alarm, thus thwarting the robbery. Video surveillance captured three men in the store, one of whom shot Nguyen presumably when he realized that she had activated the alarm. Police state that they have a good image of the gunman from the video and will be releasing photographs soon. Anyone with information regarding this crime is asked to call the San Francisco Police Department."

Jack turned off the television, dropped his head into his hands and rubbed his moistened eyes. After a moment, he called the police and mentioned that he had been in the market earlier that day but saw nothing unusual. He did say that he noted a white utility van pull into the parking lot as he was driving off. The officer told Jack that a detective would be sent to interview him sometime later in the week, though they did already have good images of the three assailants. Jack hung up and got into bed. He was distraught. *Oh my God, poor Cho,* he thought. His prayers that night were fervent.

Yet again Jack did not sleep well. His dreams were horrific, with images melding from Holly to Cho to who knows what else. He had awakened often during the night sweating and with his pulse racing. By 6:30 a.m., however, exhaustion had caught up with him and he was finally sleeping soundly. So soundly in fact that he did not hear the tumble of the lock on his door over the whirring hum of whatever machinery was operating in the warehouse below. Nor did he hear the soft steps of the intruder that had entered his room and now had a weapon leveled in Jack's direction. Quietly and with deliberation the intruder pulled the trigger, delivering the arsenal squarely into the side of Jack's face. The impact was startling as Jack felt the liquid running down his neck and shoulders. He bolted upright in bed and faced his assailant, trying to come to complete consciousness and make sense of the assault. As he wiped his eyes he identified the perpetrator and all became quite clear.

"Emily! Damn you!" Jack said as he wiped his face with his bed sheet. "Why did I ever give you a key?"

Emily sank her five foot six, 130-pound frame to the floor. Her long wavy brown hair framed her olive-complexioned face and vivid green eyes. She was holding her stomach in rigors of laughter as she cradled an Aqua Blaster 363 dual-nozzle supersoaker water gun. Jack was livid as he looked at the clock.

"Damn it Em, I told you I didn't want to go today!"

Emily caught her breath, flashed a dazzling smile, and once again aimed the gun at her adoptive brother as she delivered an ultimatum. "You can either get out of bed and come hiking with me or you can take another hit." She pumped the weapon once for effect.

Jack was undeterred. "I'm not going and don't you dare…"

Emily opened fire in a relentless deluge of pressurized water. Jack recoiled instinctively and in doing so toppled backwards off the side of his bed. It seemed as though he was falling forever, like falling in a dream. He perceived himself to be enveloped in a blue electrically charged mist, as he was barraged by a distant and muffled whirring sound. When he finally hit the ground he felt what he thought was the tremor of an earthquake. Jack pulled himself up and peered over the bed.

"Did you feel…? Em? Emily?"

Jack was alone in his room. He got to his feet and walked somewhat unsteadily around his bed. As he did so he noted that it was not soaked with water. He inspected himself and found that he too was dry.

"Emily!" he called into the empty apartment. "Come on, I'm not playing."

As Jack traversed his bedroom en route to the living room in search of Emily, he did a double take as he passed his clothes valet. His black Armani suit, the one he had worn the day before, was hanging upon it. Jack knew he had put it away. At that moment, his radio alarm went off. It was 6:45 a.m.

I know I didn't set an alarm last night, Jack thought.

Jack listened to the radio for a moment, dazed and confused.

That's the same report to which I woke up yesterday! he remembered.

He made his way to the living room. "Emily?" he called again.

When he got to the door, he saw that it was locked. Jack looked throughout his apartment. Emily was nowhere to be found, nor was there any evidence that she had been there. He was more confused as he picked up his smart phone to call her and noticed the date.

The fourth? That was yesterday, he realized.

Jack hurried back to the living room and turned on the TV. He directed the guide to Fox Business Channel. *Opening Bell* with Maria Bartiromo was airing He watched intently until he heard the date…the fourth.

What the hell is going on? Jack questioned to himself.

Jack activated his cell phone again, pulled up his favorites screen and tapped Emily's picture.

"Hello," Emily answered sleepily.

"Emily, where are you?" Jack asked hurriedly.

"I'm in bed…*sleeping*! What do you want?" Emily said, rather aggravated by the intrusion.

"How long have you been there?"

"Jack, I am a grown-ass woman. You don't have to keep up with my social life. I've been home all night. I didn't even go out last night. And before you ask, I'm alone. Goodbye!"

Emily hung up. Jack could make no sense of what was happening. *Did I dream yesterday?* he wondered. He racked his brain to remember yesterday. *Did I dream all of that?* He could make no sense of it and aimlessly began his routine of readying for the day. *I must just be exhausted,* he concluded. Jack showered and dressed in the black Armani suit that was hanging upon the valet. He poured a cup of coffee and sat down to his devotional. As he read, he knew that he had read it before. Jack had no rational explanation but convinced himself that it must truly be the fourth. *Did I not get made a partner yesterday? Is Cho all right?* Jack questioned as he descended the stairs, got into his car, and drove to work.

When Jack entered Hughes Investments, he greeted the receptionist as usual:

"Good morning, Marion."

"Good morning, Mr. Dawson. At it again early today I see," she said.

"Early bird gets the worm, right?" said Jack.

Jack smiled at Marion with a sense of déjà vu as he walked past on the way to the elevators. When the doors opened, he entered and froze when the same attractive brunette from the day before joined him. As the door began to close again, the girl turned to regard him.

"Hey there; how are you this morning?" she asked.

"Fine, thank you," replied Jack uncertainly.

Clearly he was not at all fine. They rode in silence until the elevator stopped at the tenth floor. He spoke as he exited. "Have a nice day… Bless you!"

As the door closed, Jack heard the girl emit a stifled sneeze. He cocked his head a bit and smiled in bemusement. As he had done before, Jack made his way through the complex to his private office suite. He saw Bill walking toward him.

"Coffee and doughnuts in the break room, right?" Jack asked.

Bill looked surprised. "Yeah, how did you know?"

Jack smiled and shrugged as he continued walking toward his office. When he entered his suite he saw Betty sitting at her desk.

"Good morning, Betty. Will you let Gary know I've made it in? I believe he has something to tell me." Jack gave her a wink as he passed.

Everything played out just as Jack knew it would, just as it had the day before. Gary told him that the partners loved the Hanson proposal and disclosed his promotion to partner. And, as before, Gary told Jack to take a two-week vacation. After Gary left, and he and Betty discussed the move to the fifteenth floor, Jack called his parents, again, to tell them the good news. He then made a reservation for the next night at Farallon for himself and Emily. Jack rode the elevator to the parking garage in a state of befuddlement. He got into his BMW and pulled out of the garage. As Jack drove, he glanced repeatedly at the face of his phone, waiting for it to ring. It did.

"Jack, I just got off the phone with mom!" It was Emily. "When were you going to tell me? That is *so* cool! So are you moving to Europe? Oh I hope you go to Spain. I *so* want to visit Spain! Are you moving to Spain, Jack? When do you start? I bet you're getting a *huge* raise! You know what? You're going to take me to dinner!"

Jack waited this time for Emily to catch her breath. "I'm not moving. I'm staying right here in San Francisco, at least for the time being. As for your other question, I start in two weeks; I'm on vacation until then. And I've already planned to take you to dinner at Farallon. I've made reservations for tomorrow night at eight."

"Oooo! Farallon! You *did* get a raise. Hey, since you're off…"

Jack interrupted her this time, completing her thought. "How about we go hiking in the Muir Woods tomorrow," he said. "We haven't done that since we went with Holly. It'll be a nice way to celebrate with her."

Emily was taken aback. "I think that would be great!" she said. "I'll come pick you up around 6:30 so we can get an early start. I want to get back early. I surely don't want to be late for dinner!"

Jack was actually looking forward to the outing. "Sounds great! I'll see you then. Bye Em, I love you," he said.

"Bye bye. Love you too! See you bright and early!"

Jack disconnected the call and guided his car to the Asian market.

Now, one more thing to take care of, he thought.

Jack pulled his car into the parking lot of the Dollar Store, which was adjacent to the Asian market. He parked so as to provide the best vantage point to see the entrance to the market's lot, and waited. Jack wasn't sure exactly what was going on. But, if things continued to play out as they had been, he was going to be here to make sure nothing happened to Cho.

At 3:13 p.m. he saw a beat-up white utility van pull up to the market, and three young men got out. As soon as the men entered, Jack got out of his car and moved quickly toward the market's entrance.

"Hi, fellas, how can I help you?" said Cho as the three men entered.

A tattooed, shaven-headed man approached the counter as the other two men went down either side of the store toward the back, assuring no other patrons were present. The skinhead addressed Cho. "I'm lookin for a big, kinda tall guy, comes in here a lot. Name of Jack," he said.

Cho knew exactly whom he was asking about. She had one regular customer named Jack who fit that description. He was looking for Jack Dawson. But she had a bad feeling about this guy. "Doesn't ring a bell. I get a bunch of guys in here that look like that. I don't know any names," she replied nonchalantly.

The skinhead eyed her narrowly, feeling she was not being quite straightforward. He softened his expression as he took a different tack. "Well, this guy is a buddy of mine. I just moved back into town and I'm trying to find him. He's moved since I was here last," he said.

The other two men made their way back to the front of the store. Cho was starting to feel very uneasy. "Sorry, dude, I don't know who you're talking about," Cho said.

She was pretty sure that the Jack she knew wouldn't have run in the same circle as these guys.

The skinhead looked at his partners, who nodded in return. Seeing that he wasn't making any progress with the clerk, he changed tack again. The skinhead produced a handgun and pointed it squarely at Cho's head. She gasped and jumped back. In an instant she devised a plan. She stepped up to the cash register and opened it, pulling out a stack of bills, one of which activated a silent alarm.

"Here, take the money! Just leave!" she urged, frightened.

"I don't want the money, you little bitch," said the skinhead. "You know who I'm talking about, don't you? Now tell me where I can find him or I'm gonna shoot you right between your slanty little eyes."

Jack stormed through the door just at that moment and barreled into one of the men, knocking him over into the newspaper rack. The skinhead redirected the gun toward Jack, recognizing him instantly. Jack stopped in his tracks.

"Well, look who's here," said the skinhead to Jack. "You just saved me a mess of trouble."

Jack instantaneously surveyed the situation, taking in every detail. He noted that the man whom he had knocked over was getting up to his feet; the other man had moved to position himself between Jack and the door. The skinhead addressed Jack again with a sardonic grin upon his face. "Looks like you got a problem, boy," he said. "You're in the wrong place at the wrong time."

Jack didn't feel at all apprehensive. In fact, he had played out in his mind what was about to happen as though it already had. He spoke calmly.

"I don't have a problem… But you do," he said.

Jack advanced toward the thug and as he did so, the skinhead fired his weapon. Jack saw the flash from the gun barrel and watched the bullet as it propelled towards him. With a slight twist and tilt of his head, he watched the bullet slowly pass him by. *Everything* was moving in slow motion. In fact, everyone but he appeared to be frozen in space. Jack disarmed the skinhead, twisted his arm behind his back and forced him face down onto the counter, holding the gun to the back of his head. Suddenly, all motion returned to normal speed as the two other men bolted out of the market and to their waiting van.

"Looks like your buddies left you," Jack observed. "You're not such a tough guy now, are you?"

Jack heard the squeal of tires as the skinhead's accomplices sped away, followed soon thereafter by the sound of sirens looming closer. The skinhead managed to eke out a few words.

"What kind of freak are you?" he asked.

I don't know what kind of freak I am, Jack thought to himself.

"The kind of freak that just slammed you down and ruined your day," said Jack.

Jack looked at Cho, who had pushed herself against the back counter and was looking at Jack as though she was eying a ghost. "Are you okay?" Jack asked her.

Cho stood silently, stunned.

"Cho! Are you okay?" Jack persisted.

Recovering her composure to some degree, Cho answered. "Yes, yes I'm fine… How did you do that?"

Jack ignored the question. "Did they hurt you?"

Cho stammered, "No, no I'm fine. Oh my God, you saved my life!" With that Cho sank down to the floor sobbing. Just then the police officers burst onto the scene.

"Drop the gun!" one of the officers commanded, his gun drawn and aimed at Jack, startling him.

"Wait, wait, I'm the good guy!" he urged. Jack put the gun on the counter and slid it toward the police officer while maintaining his grip on the skinhead. "This is the bad guy!" he said, tilting his head toward the skinhead. "Two others just drove off."

Cho interjected as she got to her feet. "He's right," she said. "He just saved me."

The officer calmed a bit. "All right, neither of you move," he said, then addressed his two partners. "Cuff them both," he instructed.

Once the situation was controlled the police concluded who was the criminal and who was the hero. One of the officers loaded the skinhead into the back of a squad car. The lead officer took Jack's and Cho's statements. He assured them that the other two thugs would be apprehended, and once again apologized to Jack for putting him in handcuffs. Jack reassured him that he understood, considering the chaos of the situation. When the police had left, Cho confided to Jack what she had not told the officer.

"I think those guys were looking for you," she said.

Jack looked at her incredulously. "Me? Why would they want me?" he asked.

"He said he was looking for a big guy he knew named Jack. He said that you and he were friends, and that you had moved since he was last in San Francisco. He wanted to know where to find you."

"Unless he is a client at the firm, which I doubt, I don't think he knows me. He was probably looking for some drug dealer who stiffed him. They looked like a bunch of meth-heads to me," Jack said.

"Yeah, I guess you're right," said Cho, relenting. "Well, I better call my mom and dad. They are going to totally freak! Thanks again," she said as she gave Jack a hug.

Jack waited with Cho until her parents arrived and he assured them that all was well. The police told him that he was free to go, so he walked back to his car. No one had questioned why he was parked in the next lot over. As he started his car, the Channel 9 News van pulled into the market parking lot. From it emerged Megan Hart and a camera crew. Jack was glad he was getting away from that circus.

Jack made it home uneventfully, though he was totally perplexed by the day he had just experienced. His brain hurt trying to make sense of it. To clear his mind, he went for an evening run. He didn't even try to avoid his old neighborhood; he knew that was pointless. How he longed to have Holly back. In his mind he spoke to her, telling her about his inexplicable day. When he returned home, he once again saw Steve and the two other men unloading the flatbed trailer. After Jack's crazy day, he had a feeling that he needed to be more assertive and find out what they were doing. As he approached, he noted that Steve appeared nervous.

"Hey fellas, let me give you a hand with that. It looks pretty heavy," said Jack.

Steve scrambled to block Jack's progress. "*No!* I mean, we can get it," said Steve. "Thanks, though."

Jack would not take no for an answer today and he sidestepped Steve, addressing his partners and extending his hand. "Hey, my name is Jack Dawson. I live upstairs," he said.

Tentatively and with furtive glances toward Steve, the two men stepped toward Jack.

"Hey, I'm Patrick and this is Fred," said Patrick.

Patrick had wavy brown hair and was about as tall as Jack. It appeared as though he rarely saw sunlight, judging by his alabaster skin. The other man, Fred, was about five ten, Hispanic, with short black hair. The men shook hands while Steve tried yet again to deter Jack.

"Really Jack, we can get this. But thank you anyway," said Steve. "You must be beat anyway after your run."

Patrick piped up. "Steve, it is pretty heavy. We could

use the help." Steve cut Patrick a hostile glance but Patrick was undeterred.

"Okay, sure, but just help us get it through the doorway," said Steve. "We can take it from there."

Jack helped the other men heave the pallet into the warehouse. He had never been on the first floor before. As they set the pallet down, he took the opportunity to survey the facility. It was a combination of living space and workspace, not very precisely segregated. There was a lot of what appeared to be technical and scientific equipment scattered throughout the space. It certainly was not intended for manufacturing. He saw computers, beacons, microscopes and a plethora of other high-tech equipment. It looked like a science laboratory, at least from what Jack remembered of science.

"So what is all of this stuff? Jack asked.

"It's a…well, it's for a project we're working on. An experiment you might say, you know, just fun stuff. So look, thanks again," said Steve as he ushered Jack to the door. He opened the door and shooed Jack through. "Have a good evening," Steve said. "Thanks again."

And with that, Steve shut the door the instant Jack cleared the threshold. Jack stared at the closed door for a moment, trying to process what he'd seen. He stood there thoughtfully for a moment, then turned and headed up the stairway to his apartment.

4

Emily came to pick up Jack the next morning. As Jack predicted, she was later than she said she would be; Emily was always late. He didn't mind though; it gave him time to enjoy his coffee and read his devotional. When she did ultimately arrive, they loaded into her car and drove to hike the Muir Woods.

It had been quite a while since they had really spent any time together. Jack had buried himself in work to the neglect of his family after Holly's murder. The outing was bittersweet, with Holly in both their minds while they strayed beneath the canopies of the giant sequoias. Memories came flooding back and they talked about Holly, they laughed about her and they cried about her. Jack had been happy that Emily and Holly became such good friends. Unlike with his other girlfriends, whom he'd kept mostly hidden from his family,

Jack had wanted his parents and his sister to meet Holly right away. He was so proud of her.

In a moment of silent reminiscence, Jack recalled the day that he met Holly. He was a sophomore at San Diego State and had just moved back to campus for the fall semester. Classes had not yet started, and Jack had made his way into downtown San Diego for the day. He had stopped at a small diner for lunch and was seated in a window booth. As he was finishing up his meal, rain began to fall in sheets. Jack decided to stay put until it passed and ordered a cup of coffee. Soon, he saw a harried young woman race past the window. The door to the café opened and in blew the most beautiful rain-soaked girl Jack had ever seen. Her umbrella had turned inside out and she stood at the entrance, struggling to close it. The diner was packed with people, as no one wanted to exit into the rain. The girl had no room to maneuver and after numerous apologies for jostling bystanders, she gave up and discarded the umbrella. She scanned the diner for a place at the counter or an empty table. There was none to be found. Jack had waved to her and caught her eye, motioning her over to join him in the booth. The girl had considered a moment in an effort to determine which would be the worse alternative: accept a seat at the table of a stranger or head back out into the torrential rain. She opted for the dry sanctuary and navigated her way towards the booth through the throng of people. Jack stood as she neared.

"Hey, I'm Jack," he said, extending his hand.

"Hey, I'm Holly," said the girl.

Jack and Holly had stayed in that diner together for three hours. It was as though they had known each other for years. Over the ensuing months they came to love each other profoundly. Holly had become Jack's soul mate and his refuge.

Jack's remembrance was interrupted by a gentle touch from Emily. "We better start heading back," she said.

Their emotional exhaustion was much more profound than their physical fatigue. They were relieved to sit down to a light lunch at the Muir Woods Trading Company. After a period of silence and indecision, Jack decided to tell Holly about the strange day he had experienced.

He was selective in the details that he related. Emily remained silent until after the recantation. "Don't you think it was probably just one of your nightmares?" she asked. "I mean really, you haven't had a good night's rest since Holly died."

Jack gave some credence to Emily's hypothesis. Maybe he had dreamed that Emily was in his apartment. But the rest of the day didn't make sense. "But a nightmare doesn't explain how I relived an entire day," he said. "How could I have known everything that was going to happen before it did?"

Emily pondered a moment before answering. "I don't know, maybe it was just a really profound episode of déjà vu," she said.

Jack didn't tell Emily about his encounter at the Asian

market, nor did he tell her that since his experience he was feeling stronger, more alert, and all of his senses were in hyperdrive. "Well, just forget about it. I'm sure you're right."

Just as they were leaving, Emily caught sight of a TV in the café that was broadcasting the local noontime news. She meandered closer. Jack did not notice that she had lagged behind, and by the time he got back to her, Megan Hart was speaking.

"We close our newscast with one more look at the remarkable heroism of one of our own, Jack Dawson. Take a look at this remarkable surveillance video that shows Mr. Dawson thwarting a robbery and saving the life of a store clerk," said Megan.

A grainy black and white video took over the television screen at the point where the assailant had a gun pointed close range at Jack. The gun discharged and with nearly imperceptible speed, the assailant was disarmed and subdued by Jack. The image returned to Megan Hart.

"Unbelievable," said Megan. "A true act of bravery and heroism right here in San Francisco. And exactly who is this hero, Jack Dawson? Rest assured that we will soon find out. Thanks for joining us. We'll see you back here for the six p.m. edition."

Emily wasn't the only one watching Megan Hart's report. The other patrons in the café were watching as well. Some whispered amongst themselves, having recognized Jack as the man in the newscast. Others stealthily snapped cell phone photos of him, thinking that they may have stumbled upon a celebrity. Jack's only thought was that it all seemed to happen so much quicker on the video than it did in real life. Emily stared at the screen for a moment longer before turning to her brother.

"Jack?" she asked, dismayed.

***

Andrei Gorski was a distinguished-looking man fifty-six years of age, with a full head of jet-black hair accented by white at the temples. He was Chechen, he always wore a dark suit, and he was formidable. As he sat writing at his ornate leather-topped mahogany desk, his aide entered the office.

"It's Pavkovik, sir," announced the aide.

Gorski breathed a heavy sigh before looking up with an expression of consternation. He spoke in a heavy Russian accent. "Leave me," he said. Gorski waited for the aide to exit his office and close the door behind him before he picked up the phone. "Gorski."

On the other end of the line was Demetri Pavkovik. He too was Chechen, but unlike Gorski he was balding and overweight. To look at him, one would think him to be the most benign man on the planet. One would be absolutely wrong. Pavkovik was calling from Chechnya. Now in his late seventies, Pavkovik was the Pakhan of the Obshina. That is to say, he was the boss of the

Chechen Mafia. And ruthless. Pavkovik spoke to Gorski in Chechen.

"Why can you not accomplish a simple task, Andrei?" he asked.

Gorski responded in Chechen. "My resources are limited, Pakhan," he said. "I have only local men that I have been able to manipulate to do my bidding. They were effective with the girl; I thought I could rely upon them."

"They were *lucky* with the girl, Andrei!" Pavkovik roared. "She was much too close and it took much too long to eliminate her. Now your bandits have botched this and the puppy still runs! This is unacceptable, Andrei."

Gorski cowered. "I am sorry, Pakhan. I will take care of this," he said.

Pavkovik regained his composure. "No, Andrei, I will take care of this," he said. "I am sending my best razboiniki. He will help you and he will not fail."

Gorski knew that if Pavkovik's assassin did fail, it would be he, Gorski, who would pay with his life.

"Yes, Pakhan," Gorski said.

***

On the drive home from the Muir Woods, after more thought, Jack came totally clean and told Emily everything that he had experienced the day before. He didn't try to explain the events; he clearly did not understand them. That was the reason he hadn't related the events at the Asian market during their earlier conversation. Really, he was thinking out loud, processing it all, one might say. Emily listened in bewilderment, asking only occasional questions. She was taken so off guard by what she had witnessed in the video that she didn't even know what questions to ask. The two determined that they would speak more on the topic at dinner that evening.

Emily dropped Jack off at his apartment and headed home. Meanwhile, Jack entered his apartment and lay on the sofa for a short nap. He slept well, being both physically fatigued and mentally exhausted. His phone alarm sounded at 6:00 p.m. and Jack rose to ready himself for dinner. As he walked through his bedroom to the bathroom, he heard a humming noise coming from the floor beneath him. He had become accustomed to that noise since the day he fell off his bed. Usually though, he only heard it in the early morning hours. *What is that guy up to?* Jack wondered. By the time he was out of the shower, the noise had ceased and Jack gave it no more thought. He dressed, descended the stairway and drove to pick up Emily.

Jack and Emily continued their earlier conversation over cocktails and lobster in the Jellyfish Lounge at Farallon.

"How long has this been going on?" Emily asked.

"Only since yesterday, or two days ago I guess," said Jack. "I don't know, they were both the same day to me."

Emily pondered a moment, arriving at the only possible conclusion. "You had to have been dreaming," she said with confidence.

Jack wanted to believe that, but that conclusion could not explain his day. "If it was a dream, then why do I feel so strange? I mean in a good way," Jack clarified. "I'm faster, better conditioned, sharper; I feel great."

"It's probably your adrenaline. I mean, you had a very close call, after all. You've heard about people who can lift cars when their adrenaline kicks in, right?"

"Emily, I dodged a bullet, literally!" said Jack. "Adrenaline can't explain that! I saw the bullet come out of the barrel of the gun and I side-stepped it as if it was traveling in slow motion. Everything was in slow motion! It was like I was the only one moving at all!"

Emily had no intelligent response to that. Jack took a sip of his cocktail and mused for a moment.

"It wasn't a dream and it's not adrenaline," said Jack. "Something happened to me."

Emily got the impression that he was truly alarmed. Her thought was interrupted by the ringing of Jack's phone.

"It's Mom," he said, answering the call.

"Hey Mom... No I'm fine, really. How did you hear about that? Oh, Emily told you."

Jack looked crossly at Emily, who turned away as though she was not paying attention to the one-sided conversation. "No I didn't get hurt... Really, it was nothing. I just happened to be in the right place at the right time... No, absolutely not, you do not need to come home… Dad has been in the Middle East for two weeks. He met you in New York so the two of you could relax. Enjoy your time together, everything here is fine… Okay. Tell Dad hello for me… Love you too… Bye, Mom."

Jack glared at Emily.

"What?" she innocently implored.

Jack decided to forgo this battle. "Never mind, I just wish that I had an explanation for all of this," he said. "I mean, I really do feel good, at least physically. All of my senses are even enhanced. I can see better and hear better. It's crazy."

Only one thing made sense to Emily. "Look, maybe you're just imagining all of that," she said. "You know you have been under a lot of stress lately, with Holly and the Hanson project and all."

Jack took offense at that theory. "If I'm imagining it, then how is it that I hear two women behind me talking about how your shoes don't match your outfit?" he asked.

Emily looked past Jack over his shoulder and saw two young women three tables away, leaning in close to each other in conversation. She looked down at her feet.

"What's wrong with my shoes? I paid good money for these!" she said. Emily looked doubtfully at Jack. "Wait a second," she said. "You can't hear what they're saying."

"All right, then how is it that I know that the names of the man and woman at the table behind those girls are Carl and Michelle?"

"Oh now, that is really too much," she said. "I'm throwing the bullshit flag on that one!"

With that, Emily pushed her chair back abruptly and marched to the table where the couple was seated. Jack heard her ask them their names and if they knew Jack. He chuckled at their response. Emily apologized for the interruption and made her way slowly back to her seat, but not before giving the ladies at the table next to the couple a cold, hard glare. Jack goaded her as she took her seat.

"Carl and Michelle?"

"Yep."

"And they didn't know me?"

"Nope."

Emily was becoming convinced. What was going on with her brother? "So you really did hear all of that," she acknowledged.

"I'm hearing everything; feeling everything; seeing everything; even smelling everything," Jack said. "It's a bit overwhelming. And it's becoming more profound."

"I've got it!" Emily declared. "You were abducted by aliens!"

"Really, Emily? Come on, be serious," he chided.

Emily continued her thought. "No, I'm just saying… You always hear about some guy on a farm getting beamed up to a space ship and being experimented on!" she said. "Who's to say that doesn't really happen?"

"I'm not some bubba on the farm that got abducted by

aliens and now has some robot probe up my ass! Jeez, Emily!"

Emily was somewhat hurt. "Well it's not like you have any better theory."

After a moment, Emily dismissed her indignation and became more sympathetic. "Look, you've always been fast and strong," she observed. "Maybe you're just getting faster and stronger. Maybe this thing with your senses is some kind of a gift. Maybe that thing in the store triggered something; you know, that tragic event brought it out."

Jack looked at her. "Don't you think, if tragedy brought it out, it would have happened six months ago?"

"I'm sorry, I wasn't thinking," she said. "This is just all so weird."

"I know," Jack said forgivingly. "I just wish I'd had this gift back then… Maybe I could have saved Holly. But you're right; there is something weird going on. When I fell off the bed, I was caught up in some sort of…vortex. That vortex did something to me. I just need to figure it all out… Maybe I am just stressed, and maybe it *was* all just a dream."

"Well, you know I'll help in any way I can," Emily assured him. "I'm sure it's all going to be fine, and eventually it will all make sense."

"I'm sure you're right," said Jack. "By the way, those women think I'm too good-looking for you."

Emily stared with contempt at the two women behind Jack.

"Heifers," she said.

5

Jack dropped Emily at her home after dinner and drove back to his apartment. Upon entering, he saw the flashing light of his home phone indicating that he had a message. Jack activated his voice mail. The caller was Megan Hart and she wanted Jack to call her to set up an interview. Jack knew of her, as she had reported on the murder of his wife. He never saw that coverage because he was unconscious for days after the attack. All he knew was that the crime remained unsolved.

How did she get my number? Jack questioned internally.

His new home phone number was not listed in the local directory and he had only given it to a few people. This reporter must be tenacious and apparently resourceful. Jack's mind was taxed. He decided he would worry about Megan Hart tomorrow. At that moment he just wanted to get into his bed. After a quick shower that is exactly what he did.

Jack had no bad dreams and again rested well. That is until around 5:30 a.m., when he was awakened by the now familiar droning hum coming from the warehouse below. It had recurred every morning at the same time since the day he fell off the wrong side of the bed. Normally he would register the noise and fall back to sleep. When he would awaken for the day, the sound would be absent. Something about this morning was different. The humming seemed louder and more prominent this time, more insistent, and frankly, irritating. He recalled hearing it before taking Emily to dinner last night.

What is going on down there? He wondered.

After a moment he extended his hand over the side of the bed from which he had previously fallen. As he did so, the hum intensified and he felt a sensation of static electrical charge; his hand was suddenly enveloped in a blue shimmering hue. He withdrew his hand quickly, startled by the sensation.

"Whoa!" he said aloud. He rubbed his hand vigorously to get the normal sensation to return, at the same time coming to a realization.

It was Oberman! He concluded.

Jack sprang out of bed, threw on a tee shirt, and bolted through the door and down the stairway to the warehouse door below. He began to bang urgently upon that door.

"Oberman! Open up!" Jack called. He banged harder. "Oberman!"

Steve came to the door and opened it just a slit, keeping the security chain engaged. He looked alarmed. "Jack? What's the matter? This really isn't a good time," he said.

"What the hell are you doing in there? Open up!" Jack insisted as he gave the door an emphatic kick, causing the chain to strain. Being barefoot, he immediately regretted the act.

"Doing? I'm not doing anything," said Steve firmly. "I don't know what you're talking about." Steve tried to close the door but Jack leaned in against it.

"Something is going on in there with that experiment you've got," said Jack. "Now open this door or I'm going to break it in!"

"Okay, hold on, hold on!" Steve said reluctantly. He closed the door just enough to release the chain and stepped back to let Jack inside.

As he walked in, Jack's eye was drawn to the origin of the humming. When he had previously been in the warehouse, this apparatus had not been there. Jack surmised that this was the equipment that had been on the tarp-covered pallet he helped bring in the other day. Now it was set up, exposed and activated. What Jack saw were two compact linear accelerators, although he did not recognize them as such. To him they appeared to be two lasers positioned on either side of a small cage, each aimed at the other. Two blue beams emanated from each accelerator in a horizontal orientation. As the beams struck each other, the result was a wide vertical column of atomically charged blue mist that extended from floor to ceiling and enveloped the cage situated in between. As Jack approached the apparatus, it powered down and the columnar beam collapsed. Fred and Patrick were also in the warehouse, sitting at computer terminals, looking rather sheepish as they shut down the device.

"What is this thing?" Jack asked.

"It's just a little experiment, nothing really," Steve said. "I'm sorry if the noise disturbed you."

"Well, this little experiment of yours is shooting something into my apartment and causing weird things to happen," Jack said. "So, I'm going to ask you again and if you don't tell me, I'm going to the police. Now, what is this thing?"

Steve tried to calm him. "Now wait, Jack, what kind of weird things have happened?" he asked.

Fred and Patrick stood up and moved closer to hear the conversation. Jack eyed them warily. "To start with, that blue beam is coming through my floor," he said, pointing to the spot on the ceiling that was beneath his bedroom. "A few days ago I fell into that beam and I haven't been right since."

"What do you mean? What exactly happened to you?" Steve asked, alarmed.

Jack related his experience with Emily and the water gun, and how he had fallen off the side of the bed, becoming enveloped by the blue mist. He then went on to describe the events of the ensuing day. "I had premonitions of everything that was going to happen that day.

It was as though I were living the day over again," said Jack.

Steve stared intently at Jack as he spoke. "What do you mean, you had premonitions?"

Jack struggled for the right words, knowing that anything he said would sound incredible. "Like the kind where you can tell the future."

"Oh my God," slipped from Patrick's lips.

Steve cut a hard glance toward him, and then returned his gaze to Jack. "When did this happen?"

Jack struggled to recall. "Tuesday, or maybe Monday?" he said. "I'm not sure because it's like I lived the day twice."

Steve looked at Patrick and Fred, paced for a moment, and then turned his gaze to Jack. Jack in turn looked intently at Steve and then faced the apparatus again. "Steve, you know what's going on, don't you? I can see it in your eyes," he said. "You have to tell me what this thing is. What has it done to me?"

Steve, Fred and Patrick looked questioningly at each other as Jack's attention was on the linear accelerators. Patrick shrugged, Fred shook his head no, and Steve made a decision. "Come sit down," he directed Jack. "You have to tell me every detail of what happened to you. Then, I'll tell you what this is."

The four men sat around the computer terminals as Jack related every detail of the last few days. Patrick took notes and asked details about the time frame of all the occurrences. He looked at computer graphs, charts and logarithms as Jack spoke. Fred was curious as to the physical effects Jack experienced. Steve had Jack relate the happenings again and again, prompting for even more information each time. The conversation went on for at least an hour. Finally, Patrick pulled up a particular computer graph and addressed Steve and Fred.

"You remember this spike that we thought was a power surge?" he asked. "It wasn't. This corresponds to the exact time when Jack fell into the beam. This spike is registering molecular exchange."

Fred looked at Steve who in turn addressed Jack. "Tell me again exactly what you felt when you fell into the beam."

Jack was tiring of the story. He was impatient to know what the apparatus was and what it had done to him. "Like I said, I felt a static charge and was covered in a blue electrical field of some sort," he said. "Then the ground shook like an earthquake, and when I got up from behind the bed Emily was gone."

"And you weren't there either?" asked Steve.

"What?" asked Jack, confused. "Yes, I was there, Emily was gone."

"No, that's not what I mean. Where would you have been at that same time of day the day before?" Steve asked.

"In bed asleep; my alarm goes off at 6:45 a.m.," said Jack, uncertain of the significance.

"So you didn't…and this is going to sound crazy…you

didn't see yourself sleeping in bed when you got up from the floor?" Steve asked.

"No, the bed was empty. I had just fallen out of it," said Jack, more confused than ever.

Steve turned to Patrick. "That proves it. The vibratory planes *do* overlap. Apparently at least by twenty-four hours," Steve observed.

"That's the only thing that makes sense, they would have to," Patrick concurred.

"What the hell are you talking about?" Jack asked.

"I promise I'm going to tell you everything. Please be patient a little longer," said Steve excitedly. Looking at Fred and Patrick, Steve knew that they agreed that Jack had to know. "And then you lived the day over, but this time knowing what was going to happen and changing it."

"Yeah, that's it. So tell me what happened. What *is* this thing?" he asked as he indicated the apparatus.

Steve spoke candidly. "You didn't have premonitions and you weren't seeing into the future. You weren't dreaming, either. You went back in time. One day in time to be exact. You *did* live that day over."

Jack's head was spinning. Steve deferred to Patrick, who directed Jack's attention to the apparatus. "These devices are compact linear accelerators," Patrick said. "When activated, they emit highly concentrated gamma rays at the speed of light. We have developed this device for the purpose of accomplishing molecular exchange. The day you fell into the beam, we were testing it as we had just installed all of the components." He paused to let Jack absorb the information thus far. "We were testing at the exact time you fell into the beam," Patrick continued. "We registered what we thought at the time to be a power surge. I shut the accelerators down immediately, but we couldn't find anything wrong with the system, nor evidence of a power surge."

Jack interjected, "Because I was the surge."

"Yes, you were the surge," Patrick agreed.

"Come take a look," said Steve. He led Jack to the molecular exchange apparatus; Fred and Patrick followed.

"Have you heard of Oberman Enterprises?" Steve asked.

"Sure, it's a large medical equipment supply company. My firm holds the account."

"My father is Steven Oberman, the founder and CEO. Oberman Enterprises provides a full range of products for medical application, everything from diagnostics and biotechnology to therapeutic and experimental," said Steve.

Jack wasn't sure of the connection to his situation. "So this molecular exchange apparatus is some experimental device of Oberman Enterprises?" he asked.

"Yes and no," Steve said. "My father immigrated to the U.S. from Germany as a child, just as Hitler reached the pinnacle of his rise to power. He grew up in the States remembering the atrocities he had escaped. Some in his family were not so fortunate. In 1952, my father founded Oberman Medical, which later became Oberman Enterprises. In the late 1950s, the U.S. government approached my father. He had served in the army with distinction during the Korean War. He was and is a patriot, and his country needed his help. The CIA had been active in Russia both during and after the war. Operatives there were reporting that Russian scientists were making advances in certain secret technologies, both in nuclear physics and biotechnology. They asked my father to work on their behalf to do the same. You have to remember, the Cold War was in full force at that time. Oberman Enterprises has been engaged in secret government research ever since. Many of the scientific and medical advances we enjoy today derived directly from my father's work during the Cold War."

Jack kept his eyes locked on Steve's for a moment before turning back to the molecular exchange apparatus, processing his thoughts. He looked over at Patrick and Fred before turning his attention back to Steve.

"Are you telling me that the U.S. government is building a time machine?" he asked.

Steve shook his head. "Not exactly," he said. "Are you familiar with cloning?"

Jack gave a slight nod. "Somewhat."

"Oberman Enterprises is way ahead of even the latest publicly reported advances in cloning," Steve said. "We have been sequencing and altering DNA for decades. We can modify and insert any gene into any chromosome."

"That doesn't really sound too unusual these days,"

Jack observed. "I've even read reports of that in the financial literature."

Steve nodded knowingly. "But there's more," he said. "Not only can we insert an altered gene into a chromosome, but we can also change the chromosome back to its original form by programming it to revert over a specified time period."

Steve now had Jack's full attention as he continued.

"You can imagine the implications. If the CIA targets a dictator, war lord, or terrorist leader that they want to eliminate, all they have to do is take a benign virus, mutate it to a lethal form and release it into that target's population. The target dies and the virus reverts back to a benign form. No smoking gun."

Jack was duly impressed, but he saw a major flaw in the technique. "That seems to me to be a shotgun approach," he said. "I would think that a lot of innocent people could get killed."

Steve nodded in acknowledgment. "That is a problem, and it is exactly what has happened when this technology has been used," he said. "That's where molecular exchange comes into the picture. Oberman Enterprises has been trying to figure out a way to target a mutation to a specific, isolated individual. The prototype of this device was designed to disassemble and then reassemble the entire chromosomal makeup of a living creature, as the first step to introducing a specific, lethal gene into a specific individual that will revert back to normal upon that individual's death. The ultimate goal is to accomplish this instantaneously, in real time and remotely."

"I can't imagine that would even be possible," Jack said skeptically. "It sounds like something out of Star Trek."

Steve smiled. "It is possible. We've done it at Oberman Enterprises," he said. "We can molecularly disassemble a research animal and reassemble it to its original form. We have never done it with a human, that is, until you came along."

"You mean to tell me that you scattered my molecules and put me back together?" Jack asked incredulously.

"That is exactly what I'm telling you," said Steve with a nod. "Now, during the course of this work we have discovered some side effects, which have taken my team, Patrick, Fred and myself, in a different direction. One of those side effects is that the test subject travels back in time during the process." Steve paused to let Jack absorb this bit of information. "Basically, we've stumbled across a time travel machine, and we are tasked with its development."

Jack pressed Steve on an obvious point.

"So why is this apparatus in an old San Francisco warehouse and not in some secret lab at the Pentagon?" he asked. "I mean after all, you do claim that Oberman Enterprises does secret work for the government, right? So why are you doing the work here with two guys who look like they should be in their mamas' basement playing video games?"

"It's here because the government doesn't know about

it," Steve confessed. Seeing that Jack was eyeing him questioningly, Steve went on: "Oberman Enterprises does do secret work for the government. That is, we did secret work until the current administration negotiated a deal with Chechnya."

Another puzzled look from Jack spurred Steve to elaborate further. "Let me explain," he said. "During the Cold War the CIA was watching the work that the Soviet Union was doing, and the KGB was watching U.S. advancements. When the Soviet Union broke apart, all of their research stopped and we leapfrogged ahead of them. Many of the current leaders of Chechnya were former officials in the KGB. They know that the U.S. has advanced biotechnologies. With the recent Russian aggression against Ukraine and their annexation of Crimea, Chechnya fears that they will be targeted next. They are concerned that Russia will try to bargain for U.S. biotechnical advances in exchange for a cessation of Russian aggression in Eastern Europe. But, Chechnya fears Russia would ultimately use those advances against them. To prevent that and to assure that the U.S. will intervene on behalf of Chechnya if the Russians do become aggressive towards them; they have offered to tamp down radical Islamic expansion and aggression. In exchange for that, Chechnya wants the U.S .to terminate its advancements in biotechnology so that Russia cannot get its hands upon them."

Jack didn't get the connection; this geopolitical subject matter was way out of his area of expertise. "What does Chechnya have to do with radical Islam?" he asked.

"The U.S. has long suspected that the Chechen leadership was infiltrated by the Obshina, which derived its leadership from the old KGB."

"What is the Obshina?"

"The Obshina is the Chechen Mafia," Steve said. "They have significant influence with terrorist groups such as Al Qaeda, Boko Haram, al-Shabaab, and to a growing extent, ISIS. The administration's hope is that the Chechens can influence these groups via the Obshina without it being known that they, the administration, are working with what many consider to be an Islamic terrorist group itself."

Jack's head was spinning. He wondered how he'd stumbled into this mess. "So you and Fred and Patrick are just going to continue this research on your own without the government knowing?" he asked. "Who are you guys, anyway?"

"My father is funding the work. It's important," Steve said. "He and I believe that the administration has made a terrible mistake by basically conceding to one terrorist group in an attempt to thwart others. We have to continue this work. Eventually the administration will change, and so too the philosophy toward the Obshina. As for who we are: Fred is a medical doctor and holds a Ph.D. in biotechnology. Patrick holds a Ph.D. in Physics. I have a Ph.D. in quantum physics."

Jack would never have imagined that these geeks were

so well credentialed. He considered a moment. "What about the CIA?" he asked. "Surely they don't want to see this research stop. I would think that time travel is a pretty big deal to them."

"Oh, there are plenty of people in the CIA who want the work to continue," said Steve. "The problem is that the administration has hand-picked the CIA leadership. They are in line with the President's policies full force. When they shut down the program they ordered my father to turn over all of the research data to that point. He had been warned by others in the CIA that this was going to happen. The data set that he handed over implied that our research was fruitless; a total bust. So we secretly moved the project here, out of view of administration informants. The only people who know that this work is continuing are myself, Fred, Patrick, my father and now you."

"Don't you think it a little odd that your father, a patriot, is willing to hide this work from the government?" asked Jack suspiciously.

Steve volleyed defensively: "Don't you think it odd that an administration claiming to be steadfast in the war against terrorism would make deals with terrorists? We are scientists devoted to our country. If we have gotten this far along with our research, we have to presume there is someone else who is not far behind us. That someone is likely an enemy of the U.S. If that is the case, then we have to be able to prevent them from getting this technology, or at least counter them if they already have it. "

Jack glanced around the room, then looked at Steve intently. "How do I know that you guys aren't the enemy?"

"If we were, you would most likely already be dead," Steve answered candidly. "Work with us and you'll see."

Jack walked over to the molecular exchange apparatus and ran his hand over one of the linear accelerators. He felt the static charge. An idea was forming in his mind, nascent at present, but definitely forming.

"I guess you better explain how all this works, then," he said.

6

"It's all based on molecular biology, biotechnology and quantum physics," explained Steve.

It was just after 5:00 p.m. Allegro Romano had opened for dinner. Steve and Jack sat at a secluded corner booth. Other than a few people sitting at the bar, there were no other patrons.

"Every atom, every molecule exists in a vibratory plane," Steve said, picking up where they'd left off. "The cycle speed of that vibration determines which of the infinite number of planes existing in parallel that entity occupies. The molecular exchange device demolecularizes the target entity and, we hypothesize, during that process the scattered molecules drift into a different vibratory plane. When they reassemble, they do so at a different point in time: at a time in the past."

Jack rubbed his temples, struggling to comprehend. "That is really complex," he said.

"Okay, let's take it back a bit," said Steve. He took the straw from his water glass and placed it into his glass of pinot grigio. "Look at this. What happens?"

Jack picked up on the thought immediately. "The straw appears to bend at the surface of the wine. Refraction, basic physics," he said.

"Exactly, refraction," said Steve. "That is exactly what happens when demolecularization occurs. The atomic matter is refracted from one vibratory plane, this one, into another vibratory plane, one that happens to be in the past. When we place the test subject in the cage, the longer we expose it to the beam, the greater the number of vibratory planes that are traversed and the farther back in time the subject travels and remolecularizes."

Jack was starting to grasp the concept. "So that is how you determine how far back the subject goes," he said.

Steve became animated. "That's right, but it's not a linear relationship," he said. "The refraction across vibratory planes is exponential. One second of exposure sends the target back three minutes. You were exposed to the beam for just over ten seconds, and you went back twenty-four hours."

"Why didn't I go to the future?" Jack asked.

Steve shrugged. "We don't know," he admitted. "Maybe it's not possible. Maybe past and present events are required to construct the future. Some theorize that the future does not exist. That is a question we have to study. As it stands, so far as we know we can only go to the past."

Jack took a couple of sips of his scotch old-fashioned as he pondered. That nascent idea he'd had earlier was taking form.

"How far back in time can you send someone?" he asked.

"Theoretically there is no limit. But until you, we've only been successful in sending test subjects back a few seconds," said Steve.

Jack was surprised at that revelation. "Only a few seconds?"

"We've been able to send mice back three seconds and nine seconds," Steve said. "At twenty-seven seconds the mice came back intact, but only one survived. At one minute and twenty-one seconds, all we got back was a bloody glob of flesh and bone."

Jack pushed his glass away, the image brought on by Steve's description having resulted in a sudden wave of nausea. He was becoming discouraged. "How did I make it back twenty-four hours and survive?" he asked.

Steve sat back and gazed intently at Jack. "That is what we would like to find out," he said. "The process of scattering molecules and refracting them across vibratory planes is stressful, usually lethal. The animals that were successful were the most strong and healthy of our test subject population. And we found another effect of the process. The mice that did survive became stronger. It was those subjects that were able to go back nine seconds and the one to twenty-seven seconds."

"That has happened to me! Since I went back in time

I'm stronger, sharper, and my senses are all heightened," said Jack.

Steve had suspected as much and said, "That happened because your DNA structure has been altered. We have found that each time the mice went through the process, they became enhanced in all areas of testing."

Jack started feeling better about his plan. "So if the mice get stronger each time, it seems that they should be able to travel progressively farther back in time," he opined.

"Theoretically they should, but there are two problems," responded Steve. "The basic DNA structure of the mouse allows for only a finite degree of enhancement. The genome has to be enhanced from the start. Secondly, we have to be able to decrease the exponential jump across vibratory planes. We have to be able to go back in linear increments."

"Will you be able to rectify those problems?" Jack asked anxiously.

"We can solve the problem of the time increment," said Steve. "That is just going to require some quantum formulary changes, which Patrick is working on now. The DNA modification has proven to be a bigger problem. We know how to alter genes; we don't know in what manner to alter them to allow for enhancement suitable for time travel. This is where you come into the picture. Fred wants to map your genome and study everything about your physiology, to find out how you were able to survive your journey back in time."

Jack was willing to do whatever it took to accomplish his goal.

"When do we get started?" he asked.

***

Her reputation was spot on; Megan Hart was indeed tenacious. After three more missed attempts and left messages from her, Jack finally relented and returned her call. He consented to an interview, but stipulated that it be off camera. Megan agreed to the condition and they settled upon a time and place. They met the next day, midafternoon at Backpackers Cafe and Wine Bar. They sat outside, and after getting acquainted over espresso and small talk, Megan set in to the crux of the interview.

"First, I want to tell you that I think what you did was great. You truly are a hero," said Megan.

"Well thank you, but it really wasn't that big of a deal," Jack said uncomfortably.

"Are you kidding? It was fantastic!"

"Well… Again, thank you."

Megan pulled a note pad and pen from her purse. "So, as way of background, this is what I know about you," she said. "I did some research when I reported upon the attack on you and your wife. I am truly sorry for your loss," she said sincerely.

"Thank you. That is very kind," said Jack.

"You were born in Chicago," she continued. "Your

parents, Jennifer and Ken MacKenzie died when you were five years old, and you were adopted by their close friends Max and Sarah Dawson. They moved you to San Francisco, where you grew up with them and their daughter Emily." Megan looked up from her pad. "By the way, I have been trying to get an interview with your father for years. Any chance you can help me with that?" she asked.

"Why do you want to interview him?"

"He's only the most famous federal agent since J. Edgar…" Megan realized that Jack was teasing her when she saw the impish grin materialize upon his face. "Ha, real funny," she said. "Do you know how many people would *love* to interview Max Dawson?"

"Good luck with that. He won't even talk to me about his career!" Jack said with a chuckle.

Megan leaned in close to Jack. "Is he still active in the CIA?" she asked in hushed tones.

Jack likewise leaned in conspiratorially and glanced around the terrace as though ensuring that there were no eavesdroppers. "He's retired," he whispered. With that, Jack sat back and laughed. "The most exciting thing he does now is clean his swimming pool."

Megan realized that Jack was once again teasing her. "Okay. I'm sorry, let's get back to you," she said.

Jack was actually happy for the momentary diversion. Still, Megan got back on task.

"Did you ever consider a career in the CIA?" she asked.

"I didn't really understand as a child what it was that my father did," said Jack. "My parents never steered me in that direction. I was always a numbers guy."

"What about professional sports? All state in high school track and football; football and cross country scholarships at San Diego State; and you were offered a contract to play professional baseball."

"I did okay in sports, I just never had a passion for it."

"You excelled academically too," Megan observed. "Actuarial science degree from San Diego State, graduating summa cum laude; first in your MBA class at Harvard Business School; and the youngest Senior Vice President of Domestic Trading at Hughes Investments."

"Looks like you already know everything about me," joked Jack. *Except for my recent promotion*, he thought.

Megan saw an opportunity to segue to the meat of her interview. "Obviously not everything," she said. "For instance, how were you able to pull off what you did in the market? I've watched the video over and over, and it seems to me what you did was superhuman. How can you explain that?"

Jack laughed nervously. "I wouldn't call it superhuman," he said. "I think I just had an adrenaline surge. Anyway, that video was so jumpy and of such poor quality, it made everything look like it happened faster than it really did. Like I said, it really wasn't that big of a deal."

"I've seen the video and have had it analyzed," she persisted. "The entire sequence is recorded in real time. There are no time gaps. I think there was more to it than just an adrenaline surge. What you did was truly the stuff of superheroes."

"Well, I'm certainly not a superhero," said Jack. "It was just a freak thing; once in a lifetime."

Megan registered Jack's discomfort with her line of questioning. She knew she was on to something, she just didn't know what. She was determined to keep an eye on this one. She decided to ease back on the throttle, and softened with a laugh.

"So you don't see this superhero thing becoming a habit with you?" she asked.

Jack relaxed; he was relieved that she'd stopped pushing. "Oh no, I am not cut out to be a superhero," he said. "I wouldn't want that job; I'll stick to investment banking."

7

Jack was plugged in as much as anyone ever could be. He had so many wires and tubes attached to his body that he put one in mind of a science fiction cyborg. In a corner section of the warehouse, Fred had assembled a plethora of medical and genetic testing equipment. His intent was to learn as much about Jack's genome, physiology and physique as possible, and how those attributes facilitated his successful travel back in time. Jack was on a treadmill, seemingly running with ease while Patrick stood by his side observing. Fred was sitting at a monitoring station, watching gauges and graphs and furiously jotting notes.

"How's he doing?" Steve asked Fred. He had come in to check on the status of the doctor and his patient.

"This guy is unbelievable," said Fred. "He is on Bruce protocol seven of the cardiac stress test, and has had absolutely no heart or respiratory changes. He may as well be strolling through the park licking an ice cream cone."

"So there is something special about him," Steve observed.

"Yeah, there's something," said Fred. "I'm going to bring him down," turning his attention to Jack. "All right Jack, let's cool you down," he said.

Jack gave Fred the thumbs up sign as Fred progressively slowed the treadmill to a halt and leveled out the incline. As Patrick disconnected Jack from all of the monitoring equipment, Steve and Fred pored over the data that had been obtained from the testing. Once Jack was freed from his tethers, he and Patrick joined the other two.

"How did I do?" asked Jack.

"Not bad," was Fred's blasé response.

The four men analyzed the data into the evening hours. Fred referenced various norms and Jack asked the significance of his various test results. Steve and Patrick tried to correlate those results with what they had learned about the process of molecular exchange and its time travel effect. When all was said and done, Fred decided that he needed even more information, and the team determined to begin a new round of testing early the next morning. Jack saw that this was a cautious group committed to scientific method. He would rather the process go a bit faster, though, because he had someplace he was anxious to be. Or perhaps it would be better said that he had some time at which he was anxious to be.

Jack did not go straight up into his apartment that night. Instead, he made a quick trip to the Asian market; it was another sushi and dried liver kind of night. While there, he had picked up a paper, and leafed through it as he ate in the solitude of his apartment. The second section by-line caught his eye:

Police have no leads in park slaying

For the second time Jack read a story about the murder of the mystery woman in Golden Gate Park. A sketch of a young attractive girl was revealed in the inset of the article. He read on with interest and pondered the information that was known to this point.

I wonder, he thought to himself

***

Jack was back in the warehouse for further testing at 6:45 the next morning. He spent the first twenty minutes in a tub of ice water followed immediately thereafter by thirty minutes in a heat chamber. Fred wanted to see how Jack's body responded to extreme and sudden temperature changes. He was then subjected to various alterations in atmospheric pressure and oxygen levels; all the while his physiologic response was monitored. His blood was drawn and analyzed at every stage.

When the testing session ended that afternoon, the men once again evaluated the data. Once again, Jack demonstrated very little physiological effect from the challenges.

This having been concluded, attention was turned to the work Patrick was doing on the logistics of time travel. He updated the group.

"I've worked out the issue of going back in linear increments of time rather than exponential increments. The mice are surviving more distant time travel but, as you can imagine, it is taking longer for them to reappear the farther they go back in time. In essence, they have to live that particular increment of time over again."

Jack interrupted for clarification. "So if you sent me back in time, say six months, I would not be able to get back to the present?" asked Jack.

"As of now, that is the case, but I'm working on it," said Patrick.

Jack tuned out for a moment as the conversation continued. *I'll live those six months over if it means I can live them with Holly. In fact, I wouldn't want to come back to the* present, he thought. "I would be willing to do that," said Jack, emerging from his reverie.

Steve was confused; the group had already moved on to another conversation.

"Do what?" he asked.

"Go back in time and re-live it," said Jack.

Steve and Patrick looked at each other for a moment. Clearly Jack did not understand the implications of his statement. Steve had a feeling that there was something Jack wasn't telling them. He addressed Jack. "That would not be possible," said Steve.

"Why not?" asked Jack.

"Two of the same genetic beings cannot exist in the same vibratory plane," said Steve. "If we sent you back, say six months, there would be you and the Jack Dawson of the past co-existing at the same time. That vibratory plane in which the two of you exist would not tolerate the paradox. Both you and the Jack Dawson of the past would, for lack of a better word, disintegrate. That is not just true for the six months that you seem to be interested in, but for any time farther back than seventy-two hours."

"What is so special about seventy-two hours?" Jack asked.

"Do you remember that I asked you if you saw yourself when you went back twenty-four hours in time?" Steve asked.

"Yeah, and I told you that I didn't see myself," said Jack.

"That is because vibratory planes overlap," said Steve. "Vibratory planes twenty-four to seventy-two hours in the past overlap with the vibratory plane of the present time. Overlapping vibratory planes contain only one copy of a genetic being within those overlapping planes. After seventy-two hours in the past, however, the vibratory planes are completely distinct and identical copies of genetic beings exist in each distinct plane. So, if we send you back to twenty-four to seventy-two hours in the past, there will be only one of you. If we send you back to a time greater than seventy-two hours in the past, there will be two genetically identical copies of you. The paradox would be recognized and both versions of you would begin to break down. Within a week, you would both just disintegrate."

Jack was once again disheartened, feeling that his plan to reunite with Holly was the thing that was disintegrating. Patrick registered the disappointment on Jack's face, though incorrectly concluding the reason why. He tried to reassure him.

"But like I was saying, I'm developing a portal that will allow us to send a subject back to a specific time and return that subject to the present before the paradox is recognized," said Patrick. "We just need to make sure that subject can be you."

Jack was not at all hopeful. He wanted to save Holly and then live out their lives together. He wanted to be with her, this Jack Dawson, not the Jack Dawson of the past, as selfish as that sounded. Still in his heart he knew he had to go back and save her, even if it meant that the Jack of the past would live on with her instead of him. At least he would know that in another universe she would be alive. He did feel some consolation in that.

Patrick and Fred turned back to their respective tasks. Steve took the opportunity to question Jack privately.

"Why did you agree to help us?" he asked.

"I think this is a fascinating project," said Jack. "The

science is interesting. And like you said, I'm the only subject that has been able to go back any significant length of time. It seems to me that you have no one else but me."

"You may be right; we probably don't have anyone else. But there's more to it than that, isn't there?" Steve asked. "You're charging in head first and seem to have no compunction about the risks. This 'project' could kill you. So again, why are you helping us?"

Jack wrestled for a moment with the decision of whether or not he should reveal his true motivation. He knew that he ultimately would, and determined now to be as good a time as any.

"If you could live a day over in your life and right a wrong; correct an action or inaction on your part that resulted in a terrible tragedy, wouldn't you do it?"

"What are you getting at?"

"Wouldn't you do it, even if it meant risking everything?" Jack persisted.

"Jack, it's more complicated than that," Steve said, seeing where this conversation was going. "Changing history alters the future, our present. When we send you back, if we send you back, you have to be very careful and methodical with the actions that you take."

"But the whole point of the program *is* to go back and alter the past, right?" asked Jack.

"In a very controlled way, though," Steve insisted.

"Then help me control it," Jack pleaded.

Steve saw that Jack was determined. He also saw that

Jack was shaken. "What is it that you want to do?" he asked.

Jack looked Steve squarely in the eyes. "My wife was murdered and I didn't prevent it," said Jack. "I want to go back and save her."

Jack began to relate the whole horrible incident to Steve. He had not discussed the details with anyone since his interview with the detective, conducted from his hospital bed only a week after the murder. As he recounted it, he was taken back to that fateful day. Jack, Holly and Emily had been milling about the floor at the open house of Emily's newly opened Arte del Tiempo art gallery as the last of the guests had been leaving. Holly had looked stunning and had garnered many envious stares. Jack was so in love with her and so proud of her. Though she didn't look it standing at just five foot three and 125 pounds, Holly was the perfect match for her husband with her green, deep set eyes, long brown hair, and olive complected skin. It was her heart and soul that were the perfect match.

Jack had lifted his glass of champagne and proposed a toast to his sister to commemorate her successful first show and auction. "To the success of Arte del Tiempo," said Jack. "And to Emily, the best curator of all time!"

Holly raised her glass as she pulled her husband closer. Emily curtsied in mock humility just as a security guard hired for the occasion approached.

"Ms. Dawson, the last of the guests have gone and I have secured the front entrance," he said.

Emily extended her hand. "Thank you Mike, I really appreciate your help tonight," she said graciously. "Why don't you go on home to your family, we'll lock up the back."

"Thank you, Ms. Dawson, you all have a good evening," replied the guard.

Holly excused herself to speak with one of Emily's employees before she left. Jack put down his glass of champagne and embraced his sister. "So how does it feel to be the owner of the most prestigious art gallery in San Francisco?" he asked.

Emily giggled. "We're not quite there yet, but it feels great!" she said. "I was *so* nervous."

"I had no doubts, Em," said Jack.

"Thanks for being here," Emily said. "It meant so much to me to have the two of you with me tonight."

Jack released his sister and stepped back, taking her hands into his. "We wouldn't have missed it for the world," he said.

Having said her goodbyes, Holly returned to her husband's side. "Break it up, you two. People are going to think that you are lovers," she said, laughing.

Jack let Emily's hands fall and pulled his wife toward himself.

"Let's get out of here and I'll show you who my lover is," he said.

"Ooo, that sounds like fun!" said Holly with a sultry smile.

Emily feigned disgust. "Ugh! Gag me! You guys are *so*

gross," she said. "You would think that after being married for almost five years you would have gotten that out of your systems. Get out of here you two, before I call vice!"

Holly gave Emily a big hug. "You did great tonight!" said Holly. "I'm so happy for you."

"Thank you. And thanks for tearing that big nerd away from work to be here," said Emily, nodding toward her brother.

"Believe me, he wouldn't have missed it for the world," said Holly. "He has been so nervous that something was going to go wrong tonight. He's been obsessing over it."

Emily looked over Holly's shoulder to Jack as she addressed him. "Really! No doubts, huh? You big liar," she said, laughing.

Holly released Emily and turned to Jack. "So much for your premonitions," she said jokingly. She walked over to him and entwined her arm in his. "Come on lover boy, let's go home," she said.

Jack gave Emily a kiss on the cheek. "Bye. I'll call you tomorrow," he said.

Jack and Holly made their way to the rear of the gallery and out the back door into the alley. As the door swung shut, it latched behind them. It was a cold night and Holly huddled next to her husband as they walked down the alley toward the main street fronting the gallery. Halfway down, three figures emerged from the shadows some distance ahead of them. Jack, knowing that the door to the gallery had locked behind him, decided to press forward toward the main street. Holly noticed them too.

"Jack, what…?" she started to ask.

"Just keep walking, baby," Jack instructed.

The men spread out as they walked toward Jack and Holly, effectively blocking the alley. It wasn't until the three were upon them that Jack could see well enough to realize they were wearing ski masks. The apparent leader addressed them.

"Well looky what we got here," he said. "We got us a couple of high-class artsy-fartsies. And look at this pretty little thing," he said referring to Holly

He then produced a gun and pointed it at Jack's head. Holly gasped. One of the accomplices pulled a knife and rounded behind Holly, grabbing her by her hair, holding the knife to her throat. Holly froze. Jack tried to defuse the situation.

"Look man, we don't want any trouble," he said. "Here, take my wallet, there's plenty of cash in it." Jack slowly and methodically removed his wallet from his back pants pocket and tossed it at the feet of the gunman. "And here, my watch. Take my watch. It's a Rolex," he said. Jack unclasped the watch and tossed it as well.

The gunman picked it up to admire it. "That's real nice of ya," he said. "Looky here boys, we got us one of them charitable snobs."

The two other thugs laughed.

"That's all that we have, now let us go on our way," implored Jack.

As the gunman put the watch and wallet in his jacket pocket, he eyed Holly. "Oh no, you got one more thing that I want," he said.

That was all that Jack needed to hear to spur him into action. He made his move and lunged toward the gunman. As he did so, Jack saw a flash followed by a deafening crack. Somewhere behind him he heard Holly's scream as his knees buckled and he fell to the ground. He couldn't catch his breath and as he clutched at his chest, warm blood coated his hands. The last thing that Jack saw before losing consciousness was the image of Holly being dragged into a darkened nook of the alley. When Jack had regained consciousness three days later in the hospital, he learned that Holly had been raped and killed. He had been left for dead.

Jack was exhausted after recounting the rape and murder of his wife. Steve had no idea that this was the story Jack would tell. He was shaken. "I told you that you had to be careful about altering history," said Steve. "To me, Holly's death was the alteration in history. You need to fix it. We'll get you there."

The seed of doubt that had been in Jack's brain for so many months was gone. He knew that soon, he would have his beloved Holly once again in his arms.

8

Jack let himself into his parents' home. The couple had returned from their vacation to New York City and invited Jack and Emily over for supper.

"Mom? Dad?" Jack called out.

"In the kitchen, baby," said Sarah.

Jack joined his mother in the kitchen and greeted her with a kiss. Sarah Dawson was a comely woman in her mid-sixties. She had light brown hair, her color of choice, and deep-set dark eyes. She came up to Jack's chest and was a bit plump. Still, she appeared and acted younger than her age.

"Hey, Mom," said Jack.

Max Dawson entered from the back patio wearing a grilling apron. "There he is, my son the hero!" he said.

Max engulfed Jack in a bear hug. And Max Dawson was a bear of a man. A little shorter than Jack at six feet, he was built like a tank. Also in his mid-sixties he, like his wife, appeared younger. The only clue to his age was his stark white hair. His blue eyes were as bright as ever.

"Feeling solid, son, you must really be working out. You get that physique from your parents." Max regretted saying it immediately. "I'm glad that you were able to put that bad boy down," he quickly added in the hope that Jack would not register his previous comment.

"I'm sure you would have done the same thing," said Jack.

"I sure would have tried!"

Jack had no doubt that Max Dawson would have succeeded. He had never known anyone braver, smarter and stronger than he.

"How was your trip to Afghanistan? Are you sure that you're retired?" Jack asked.

Max laughed. "One never really retires from the CIA. But as much as can be possible, I am retired," he said. "I'm doing some occasional consulting. I really like President Ghani. You know I worked with him before, when he was a special advisor to the United Nations."

"Really; I didn't realize he had worked with the UN. I just know of him from his work with the World Bank," said Jack. "So, how was New York?"

"We loved it. It was a nice little vacation," Max said.

Jack noticed that Emily had not yet arrived. "Where's Em?" he asked.

Sarah feigned exacerbation. "Have you ever known your sister to be on time for anything?"

"You've got a point there," said Jack.

Max Dawson grabbed a Dos Equis from the refrigerator for himself and handed one to Jack. "Come help me out back with these steaks, son," he said.

Max and Jack went onto the back patio, where Max had a top of the line outdoor kitchen. He spoke as he turned the steaks. "I'm real proud of you, son. I know that you're going to make a real difference with your new venture."

Jack became nervous. *Did he know?* he wondered. "My new venture?" he asked.

"International investment banking, son, you're going to be great at it!" Max said.

"Oh yeah, I'm really looking forward to it," Jack said, relieved. He paused a moment, thinking back on what Max had told him inside. "Dad, you said that I got my physique from my parents. Were they in good shape? Was there anything unusual about them?"

Max felt a pang. *Damn it*, he thought. He was uncomfortable with this line of questioning but he didn't let it show. He had regretted his earlier statement about Jack's parents as soon as he had said it, but hoped that Jack wouldn't register the comment. He did.

"Jennifer and Ken were in great shape. Very fit. They had excellent genes, obviously passed on to you. Why do you ask?" Max probed.

"No reason, just curious," said Jack dismissively.

Max wasn't convinced. Jack took a sip of beer.

"Do you know the Director of the CIA?" Jack asked.

"Yeah, I know him," said Max.

"Is he any good?"

Max was becoming quite suspicious now. *Why are you suddenly interested in this, son?* Max wondered. "He was a good choice for this President," he said.

"How so?" Jack asked.

"He'll do as he is told," said Max.

"So, you don't think he is good for the CIA?" Jack asked.

"He's a political appointee, son," said Max. "He has no real connection to the CIA other than as a bureaucrat. I just hope that some of the old boys can keep things together until he moves on." He poked the meat one last time.

"This is ready, let's eat!" Max said.

It wasn't ready, but Max was ready to terminate their conversation on this topic.

***

Jack was back in the warehouse at seven the next morning. As he entered, Jack saw Patrick laboring over what looked like a wristwatch, and a small box-shaped item that Jack could not decipher.

"Hey, come take a look at this," said Patrick upon noticing Jack's arrival.

Jack ambled over as Patrick pushed his stool back to give Jack an unencumbered view.

"So what do you think?" Patrick asked.

Jack studied the items. "I think you've got a roach hotel and a Cracker Jack watch," said Jack facetiously.

Patrick was offended. "The 'roach hotel' is a targeting device," said Patrick. "This device is going to place you at an exact location when you travel back in time. The 'Cracker Jack watch' is your polarization band."

Steve emerged from the kitchen with two cups of coffee. He handed one to Jack and took over the conversation, having heard it from the start.

"Good morning," he greeted Jack. "I'll explain to you how these devices work." Steve took the targeting device in his hands. "This is a quantum targeting device," he said. "It will allow us to direct the quantum portal to a particular location at any time in the past. It's the 'homing device' Patrick has been working on. When we activate the demolecularization beam, a quantum portal opens in the time-space continuum. When you refract to the past, your molecular energy will be directed to wherever we physically place this device."

Steve placed the targeting device back onto the workbench and lifted the polarization device. "This is a quantum polarizer," he said. "Wearing this will allow you to access the quantum portal at the location of the targeting device."

"So what will I do with them?" Jack asked.

"Patrick has solved the problem of getting you back to a specific point in time within seconds of our target time," he said. "When the demolecularization beam is activated, the quantum time portal will open at the physical site of the targeting device. The chip in the polarization band has been programmed to specifically align the energy of the quantum portal to match your molecular energy, so that only you can pass through. In other words, the portal's vibratory rate will be synchronized with yours regardless of how far back in time you go. You must be wearing the band to access the portal. Otherwise we will not be able to get you back into the portal and to the present."

Jack studied the devices. "Will I be able to see the portal?" he asked.

Patrick took this question. "I'm developing glasses that will allow for that," he said. "But you are going to have to know the general location of the targeting device in order to find the portal. Look here."

Patrick indicated a knob on the polarization band. "When you are wearing the glasses and are within fifty meters of the portal, push this knob in and the portal will become visible to you as bluish distortion in space," he said. "As you get within three meters of the portal, the polarization band will reconfigure the portal's polarity to match your energy and let you through. Once you pass through, the portal will once again become invisible until it is shut down.

"You guys are amazing," Jack said, awed.

"There is one small catch," Steve said. "We can only keep the portal open for thirty minutes at most. After that it becomes unstable and will begin to break down."

"So that means I can only stay in the past for thirty minutes?" Jack asked.

"I'm afraid so," said Steve.

"That's not very long," said Jack, mostly to himself.

Patrick directed Jack's attention once again to the polarization band. "The LCD panel will indicate how much time you have to re-access the portal," he said. "Additionally, the band functions as a transtemporal GPS. We will be able to see your physical location in the past. I'm also working on a device so that we can talk to you in the past. I just have a few kinks to work out."

Jack's head was spinning. "So I'm going to be able to talk to you in the present from the past?" he asked.

"Exactly, the communication device will be built into your disguise," said Patrick.

Jack's head popped up. "What disguise?"

At just that moment Fred entered the warehouse with laptop in hand. "He's ready!" said Fred. "Everything looks great. He just keeps getting stronger and stronger. We are green light to go!"

Jack barely registered Fred's remarks. "No one said anything about a disguise," he said. "Why would I need a disguise?"

"Patrick, as soon as you're ready with the equipment, we'll send Jack back in the first increment," Steve said excitedly.

In a very loud voice Jack repeated his question. "Are you guys giving me a costume? You've got to be kidding me. I don't want to dress like some comic book super-hero! Come on!"

Fred looked at Steve. "I told you that he wasn't going to like it," he said.

"Jack, we talked about this," said Steve.

"I didn't hear any talk about a costume!" Jack replied.

"You know what happens when we send you back more than seventy-two hours," said Steve. "There will…"

"I know that I'm not wearing a costume!" Jack declared.

"There will be a Jack Dawson of the past," Steve went on. "We can't risk you being seen by someone who knows that Jack Dawson, much less being seen *by* that Jack Dawson."

"Well then, we'll just have to make sure that I'm nowhere around me!" Jack said.

He was taken aback by the absurdity of his own statement. Jack closed his eyes and shook his head to clear his mind. Steve allowed him to process the information, knowing that in time he would come to understand the need for a disguise.

"So what does this costume look like, a bodysuit and red cape?" Jack asked sarcastically.

"It's a disguise, not a costume," said Steve patiently.

"So what does this disguise look like then?" Jack pressed.

"The undersuit is made of etartenepon," responded Patrick.

"Oh, well that clears it up nicely," said Jack with sarcasm.

"The etartenepon suit will conform to your body, allowing for full range of motion while helping to maintain a constant core body temperature and preventing any degree of penetration," Patrick replied.

"What do you mean, 'prevent penetration'?" Jack asked suspiciously.

"We have to have you prepared for any eventuality," said Steve. "You are going to be a man in disguise appearing out of nowhere. Someone may feel threatened and take action, like trying to shoot or stab you. Additionally, if you are ultimately going to do what you plan to do with regard to Holly, you are going to be in a very dangerous situation."

Jack did see reason in that. Patrick continued:

"Etartenepon is like a supercharged Kevlar," he said. "It is impenetrable not only to bullets and knives, but also to heat, cold, water, everything." Patrick spoke with pride, having developed etartenepon; it was his baby.

Jack was impressed, but still curious. "So I presume that I'm not going to be just running around in some leotard," he said.

"No, you'll wear a disguise over it," said Patrick, somewhat offended.

"So what exactly do you have in mind for my 'disguise'?" Jack asked tentatively.

"That's what you and Patrick have to decide," said Steve.

***

Jack thought about his "costume" during his run. He couldn't imagine what was in store for him but he knew that Patrick was a Marvel Comics fan, and felt that would not bode well for him. His mind's eye kept seeing images of himself wearing a unitard and cape, putting him in mind of a preposterous superhero. He tried to shake the image from his mind by returning his thoughts to Holly, whom he hoped to see soon. In fact, he was so focused upon Holly that this time he made a conscious decision to run by their old home and was actually uplifted by the prospect.

At the moment, however, Jack was traversing Chinatown, a good distance away from Russian Hill. As he rounded a corner and began an uphill assent, Jack saw a young woman bound out of a hastily parked car and run toward a shop. It was near closing time. In her oblivious rush, she did not notice the car begin to roll backwards down the street. In a flash Jack traced the trajectory of the car, noting an old woman struggling with a vegetable cart in its path. He bolted and though some distance away, he was upon the woman in an instant. Just as he swept her away, the runaway car pummeled her cart before crashing into an adjacently parked car.

A crowd of people was upon them at once to attend the old woman. Soon her husband heard the commotion and emerged from his shop. Seeing that his shaken wife was at the center of the bustle and having been told of the near tragedy averted by the stranger, he thanked Jack profusely, bowing repeatedly. The group of bystanders upon the scene all marveled at the speed and agility that Jack had demonstrated in the course of the rescue. One of the bystanders recognized him.

"Hey, you're Jack Dawson, the guy from the robbery video!" he announced.

"Man, you were moving like lightning," remarked another.

Jack was beginning to feel uncomfortable with the attention and the recognition. "Well, you know, adrenaline," he replied.

Jack assured the old lady that she was going to be fine and began to back away from the throng as they pressed in upon him. Finally breaking away, he escaped at a run up the hill. A third bystander called after him as the crowd applauded.

"Hey, Jack Dawson, you're a superhero! Way to go, man!" he said.

As Jack made his way toward Russian Hill, he ruminated on the old lady's rescue. Why was he there at just that moment? What had drawn him to Chinatown anyway? He rarely ran through that area. He let those thoughts go as he neared his old home. He slowed his pace and smiled as he ran by. He promised Holly that he would be coming for her soon.

Jack was feeling wonderful as he finished his run. He climbed the stairway and let himself into his apartment.

He grabbed a bottle of water from the fridge, and just as he settled in his phone rang.

"Hello."

"Jack, Megan Hart here. You did it again," she said. "You're making quite a name for yourself."

"I beg your pardon?" Jack asked, not understanding her comment.

"Another random act of heroism, all of Chinatown is talking about it."

"Megan, I wouldn't make a big deal of that," said Jack. "I was…"

"Let me guess; you were in the right place at the right time," said Megan, completing Jack's sentence.

"Exactly, that's all there was to it," he said.

"Well, Jack, I don't know about that. I have my hands on a cell phone video of the whole thing. It seems to me like it was a very big deal. The only problem is that you're a blur in the video."

"Well, those cell phone videos aren't of very good quality."

"Oh that's not what I mean," said Megan. "The video quality is fine. The problem is that you were moving so fast that your image is just a blur. What do you make of that?"

Jack didn't know how to respond. "I don't really know what you're talking about," he said after a pause.

"Tune in to the Ten O'clock News tomorrow and you'll see what I'm talking about," she said. "I've got my eyes on you, Jack Dawson." With that, Megan hung up the phone. Jack closed his eyes and shook his head slightly.

This is not going to be good, he thought.

9

Jack and Emily were seated outdoors at Farley's on Portrero Hill, just down the street from Emily's art gallery. Jack recounted the events surrounding the old lady with the vegetable cart in Chinatown.

"I wasn't even planning to be there," said Jack. "I just started running and that is where I ended up. It was as though I was drawn there."

"Maybe whatever is going on with you really is a gift," said Emily. "Maybe you should embrace it and see where it takes you."

Jack sipped his mocha latte. "Do you remember, I told you I was going to figure this thing out?" he asked.

"Did you?" Emily asked in return.

"I did. Well, for the most part did," answered Jack. "It's a work in progress."

Emily looked at Jack imploringly. "And?"

Jack took another sip as he contemplated. "I'm not

quite ready to tell you about it," he decided. "It's pretty farfetched, but once I piece it all together, I think you need to know."

"Does this have anything to do with Holly?" Emily asked.

"It has everything to do with Holly," admitted Jack.

"Look, I'm ready to hear about it whenever you're ready to tell me. Just don't get hurt any more than you already have been," she said.

"Thanks for not pressing," said Jack sincerely.

They sat in silence for a bit, drinking their coffees. Jack was lost in his thoughts of Holly and Emily was lost in concern for her brother. Jack broke the silence.

"I want to go back to the gallery," he said.

Emily was hesitant to agree. She knew the trauma that Jack associated with her place. He had not been back to Arte del Tiempo since the night that Holly was killed.

"Are you sure?"

"Yeah," said Jack. "I'm ready."

Emily smiled. "When do you want to go?"

"How about now?"

Emily searched Jack's eyes for a moment. *Is this really a good idea?* she questioned to herself. Emily decided to take the chance. "Okay then, let's go," she said.

Jack and Emily strolled down the street to her art gallery and entered its spacious foyer. Just a few patrons were milling about at that early hour. Emily introduced Jack to her staff as she escorted him throughout the premises and the current art exhibit. A lot had changed since he had been there last. Emily had added decor that gave the gallery a more Romanesque element.

"This place really looks great. You should be very proud," said Jack.

"I am proud," Emily confessed. "I really love what we're doing here. This is who I am. This is Emily Dawson."

One of Emily's staff members cornered her, as he needed help with an issue pertaining to the upcoming exhibit. Jack reassured her that he would be fine as she went off to attend business. He wandered around the gallery, remembering that last date he'd had with his wife. His recollections were fond, probably because he knew that he would soon have Holly back. Emily returned after a bit and she and Jack continued their exploration of the gallery. When Jack readied to leave he asked Emily if it would be all right for him to exit out the back door.

"Jack, do you think that is a good idea?" she asked with concern.

"I think I need to," he said.

Emily walked Jack to the back and bade him farewell. Jack exited and rounded the corner into the alley where he was attacked and Holly was killed. The memory was harder to tolerate than he had anticipated. Still, he reconnoitered the street, taking in every minute detail, all the while hearing Holly's soft distant voice in his head. He responded to that voice.

I'm coming, baby, just hold on a bit longer, he said to himself.

Jack made it a point to be home in time to watch Megan Hart and the Ten O'clock News, nervous about what he might see. Finally, she presented the story of the Chinatown rescue.

"And now we have another story in the Jack Dawson saga," said Megan. "As you may recall, Jack Dawson was the hero of the Asian market robbery where he saved the life of a store clerk. Well, yesterday our superhero was at it again."

Jack cringed at the term.

"Soo Chan Lee, a well-known vegetable merchant in Chinatown, was his latest rescue," said Megan. "Take a look at this cell phone video."

The image changed from that of Megan Hart to a replay of a tourist's cell phone video footage. The tourist was spanning the shops of Chinatown when Jack's blurred image zoomed through the frame. It took a moment for the tourist to recapture the blur racing toward an old woman struggling with a cart as a runaway car descended the hill toward her. The video captured Jack scooping up the old lady just as the car crashed into her cart, obliterating it. The TV image changed once again to Megan conducting on-site witness interviews.

"Tell me what you saw here today?" Megan asked one woman.

"It was amazing. This guy just comes out of nowhere

like a flash. If it hadn't been for him, that woman would have been crushed!" she said.

"It was all so fast," said a young black man. "I never really saw the dude until it was all over! That homie can move! He was like Flash Gordon or something."

The image on the screen transitioned back to Megan Hart in the newsroom.

"That's our news for tonight," she said. "Good night, San Francisco, and good night to you, Jack Dawson."

Jack turned off the TV and sat for a moment in silence. *I knew this wouldn't be good*, he thought.

It did not take long before Jack's phone rang. It was Emily.

"Hey, Em."

"Okay, now you've *got* to tell me what's going on!" Emily said.

***

Every night before they settled into bed, Max and Sarah Dawson watched Megan Hart and the Ten O'clock News. Tonight was no different. Max sat forward in his recliner and rubbed his face with both hands after having seen the report describing Jack's rescue of the old lady in Chinatown.

"Max…" Sarah spoke first.

Max sat up and looked at his concerned wife. "I know," he said. "I'll tell him. He has to know."

Max pondered, rubbing his temples to ward off an

oncoming headache. After a moment he picked up his phone and scrolled through his contacts. Sarah knew that Max wasn't going to tell Jack over the phone. She knew for whom he was searching. Max found the number and placed the call.

"Hello Steven, this is Max Dawson. I'm sorry for calling at such a late hour." Max paused. "Yes, it has been a very long time. Look, something has come up; we need to talk. Can you meet with me tomorrow at 1300 hours?" Max paused again. "Yes, I'm afraid so." Max listened to the voice on the other end. "Okay then, I'll pick you up tomorrow at 1300. Goodbye."

Max hung up the phone and looked at his wife. She registered his unease.

"We knew we would have to tell him sometime," Sarah reminded Max gently.

Another viewer was watching the news that night as well. It was Andrei Gorski, and he was losing patience. He picked up his phone and placed a call. He spoke in Chechen.

"Nicolai, I want you at my office tomorrow morning," said Gorski. "This thing must be done soon."

Without waiting for a response, Gorski disconnected the call. He knew that Nicolai would be there at the appointed time.

***

By the time Jack walked into the warehouse the next

morning, the rest of the team was already assembled. Fred and Steve were poring over Jack's physiologic and genetic test results while Patrick tinkered with some apparatus. It was Patrick who saw Jack first and spoke. "Hey, it's Flash Gordon!" he said.

Jack cringed. Obviously Patrick had seen the news report. Steve and Fred turned and Steve shot Jack a look of disapproving concern. "Jack, you cannot…"

"I know, I know," Jack interrupted. "Look, I wasn't even planning on being in Chinatown. It just happened. What was I supposed to do, just let that old woman get run over?"

"Of course not," said Steve. "It's just not a good idea for you to draw attention to yourself, especially not now. If Megan Hart starts to dig into you and finds out what it is that we are doing, we will lose everything. She is a bulldog."

"I know; I realize that," he said. "I understand how important all of this is to you guys. It's important to me too, maybe for different reasons, but I don't want our work jeopardized either." He paused and looked the group over. Throughout the night he had tried to make sense of everything that was happening to him.

"Look, I don't at all understand what is going on with all of this. I paced the floor all night trying to make sense of it, trying to find the purpose in it. I've thought about it; I've prayed about it; I've meditated upon it; I even went as far as to talk myself out of it," said Jack. "But the truth is this: Ever since Holly died I've been wandering around aimlessly. I threw myself into my work, but I still felt lost. I feel now that I have a purpose. I saved Cho. I rescued that old lady. It is for those reasons that all of this is happening. It's not just about me saving Holly, though of course I want that more than anything. I believe that all of this has happened because I am meant to help anybody in danger; save lives, right wrongs."

Jack paused again in thought. His audience remained attentive.

"I know that I am called to do this work and I know that you guys are a part of it," continued Jack. "I can't do it without you. This all seems so familiar to me. You all seem so familiar to me. It's as though I have known you guys forever. I don't believe that it was by chance that I moved into the upstairs apartment. It's not serendipitous that, for whatever the reason, I am able to survive time travel. There is a force at play stronger than any one of us that has instilled in me this sense of mission. "

Jack's discourse was heartfelt and compelling. Somehow, they all felt it too. And though no one had verbalized it before Jack, they all had felt that same sense of mission deep in their souls. They knew that they had become something bigger than themselves. They all knew, without having spoken a word about it before, that Jack was right. Some larger force was not only driving them, but was also enabling them.

"Then we best figure out how to get you to where and when you need to go," said Fred.

Jack was relieved. He'd been afraid that his newfound friends would think him absurd.

"I promise, from here on out I'll keep a low profile," he said. "So, with that in mind, what's the status of my disguise?" He had come to see just how important it was to operate incognito.

"Patrick has gathered a selection for you," said Steve.

"You are going to be one stylin' superhero, my friend," said Patrick, lightening the mood.

Jack cringed again. "Okay, that's enough with the superhero stuff, guys."

The group laughed as Patrick stood to lead Jack to view his assortment of disguises. "All right, Batman, come with me and we'll see what you think of these," joked Patrick. Jack just shook his head in dismay and followed.

In a makeshift dressing room Patrick had assembled various items of clothing. First, he handed Jack the etartenepon bodysuit, now complete with matching gloves. "Go behind that screen and put this on," directed Patrick, indicating a free-standing dressing screen. Jack ducked behind it.

"This is the etartenepon bodysuit? Looks like you made special feety pajamas," said Jack.

"Those special feety pajamas are going to save your ass one day," said Patrick, slightly affronted. "Just put it on. Your disguise will go over it."

Jack put on the bodysuit and tried various disguises over it. The first choice was a polyester jogging suit that put him in mind of Richard Simmons. The next was a cobalt blue biking suit with red swooshes down the sides. "Oh yeah, I'll really blend in with this one," said Jack sarcastically.

Next was a black suit complete with hat and sunglasses, straight out of *Men in Black*. "Been done already," observed Jack.

After a few other failed attempts, and resorting to mixing and matching various components, they finally found Jack's look. Patrick emerged from the dressing room first and garnered the attention of Steve and Fred, who were once again attempting to make sense of Jack's test results.

"You guys are going to love this," he said as he approached them. "Come on out, Jack!"

Jack emerged from the dressing room. On his feet were sleek black boots into which were tucked black, multipocketed Special Forces type pants. He wore a black form-fitted crew neck shirt under a futuristic long black duster. The ensemble was completed by the gloves, wraparound sunglasses, and a black beret. The effect was impressive, and best of all, Jack was unrecognizable. Patrick was quite pleased with himself.

"Gentlemen, I present Quantum Man!" he declared.

Steve and Fred laughed at the joke. Jack yet again cringed at the superhero reference. Patrick began to explain the suit.

"Jack has the etartenepon bodysuit underneath. All of this," he said, indicting Jack's disguise, "will also be reinforced with etartenepon. The glasses will be fitted with polarization lenses and quantum spectra vision. He'll have an earpiece built into the arm of the glasses to hear communications from us, and a microphone built into the lapel of the coat to talk to us. I'll have it ready in a couple of days and will then teach him how to use everything."

"Sounds to me like you're going to be Inspector Gadget," said Fred.

"Really? Not you too!" Jack said.

"All right, Jack, you get out of that suit and Patrick can start working on it. Fred and I need to go over your test results with you," said Steve.

***

Nicolai Popov was a big olive-skinned, handsome Chechen in his mid-thirties, with dark wavy hair and striking sea-blue eyes. He sat across from Andrei Gorski in Gorski's lavish office. Again, they spoke in Chechen.

"This leaves no doubt," said Gorski. "It has happened just as Pavkovic has feared. There is no room for error. You must not fail."

Nicolai exuded confidence. "I have never failed," he assured Gorski.

***

When Jack reemerged in his street clothes, he found

Steve and Fred huddled around the computer at Fred's workstation. Jack made himself a cup of coffee and walked over to join the two. Steve directed Jack's attention to a large flat-screen TV to which Fred had linked his computer, motioned to Jack to take a seat to view the TV, and followed suit.

"Take a look at this," said Steve. "Fred has compiled the results of all of the physiologic and genetic testing that he has put you through."

Fred presented a grouping of plot graphs and bar charts. "In every instance, with every scenario, and under every stressor, you progressed through each test with no perceivable physical or physiological degradation," said Fred. "In fact, you have progressively strengthened."

"So what do you make of that?" Jack asked.

"We couldn't make anything of it until we mapped out your genome," said Fred as he clicked two new images onto the screen. "The image on the left is a map of your genome. The image on the right is a computer generation of an ideal genome that was drawn from elite athletes, scientists and world leaders. In essence, the ideal genome is free of any irregularities or blemishes, neither deletions nor insertions nor mutations. A person with this genome would have exceptional physical, cognitive and sensory abilities with the potential to master any physical or mental pursuit."

Jack studied the two images closely. "I don't see any difference," he said.

"That's because there isn't any difference, at least none of significance," said Fred.

"So what does all of this mean?"

"It means that with very little exposure, you can master anything you choose, whether it be athletics, music, literature or even quantum physics," said Steve.

Jack was incredulous. "I can't do those things," he said. "I was always a pretty good athlete and I know finance, but I've never done anything with music or science or anything else, for that matter."

"Just because you haven't done something doesn't mean that you can't do it," said Steve.

Jack sipped his coffee as he tried to take in this bombshell of information. "Did the molecular exchange beam alter my genetic makeup when I went back in time?" he asked.

"No, it was your genetic makeup that made it possible for you to travel back in time and survive," said Fred. "As far as we know, you were born with this exceptional genome."

"Jack, how much do you know about your parents?" asked Steve.

"I was young when they died, so not much," said Jack. "My father, that is, my adoptive father, did say that they were both in very good shape."

"We need to learn more about them. The chance of you being born with this genetic makeup from your parents without it having been manipulated in some way is astronomical," said Steve. "As it stands right now, you are the only being who can survive time travel. We need to know why."

Jack left that encounter with Steve and Fred feeling totally overwhelmed and frustrated. He just didn't know very much about his parents. When he asked about them as a child, Max and Sarah gave him basic information, but they were not very detailed. Young as he'd been, that was good enough for Jack at the time. Jack realized now, however, that Max and Sarah had been rather evasive. Why hadn't he asked more questions, he wondered. Did he just not care? Was he too young to care? Jack needed some answers and he needed counsel. He got into his car and began to drive. As he did so, he called his sister.

"Hello," Emily answered.

"Hey, are you busy?"

"Busy sitting on my butt."

"You feel like going for a drive?" Jack asked.

"Sure, what's up?"

"I need to tell you what's been going on."

"Well, okay. Come pick me up," said Emily.

"I'll be there in fifteen minutes," said Jack.

Jack ended the call and directed his car to Emily's house. He arrived fifteen minutes later and the two loaded themselves back into Jack's car. They drove up the ocean road, initially in silence. Emily didn't press Jack to explain what was going on with him; she knew he would start the conversation. In time, Jack pulled off the road and parked at an ocean view lookout. They got out of the car and made their way down the bluff to an observation platform that was situated at the edge of a cliff. Below them the ocean waves crashed upon the rocks.

"I need to tell you something," Jack said.

"Sure, what is it?"

"It's going to sound like I'm crazy."

"What's new?" said Emily with a laugh, attempting to lighten the mood.

Jack diverted his gaze from the crashing waves and looked at Emily. "I'm being serious, Em."

"Okay, I'm listening," she said. "What's going on?"

Jack related to Emily everything that had transpired, from his initial jolt back in time to the present moment. He told her how he confronted Steve Oberman, and about all the testing he had gone through and the results of those studies. He explained to her everything that he knew of the molecular exchange apparatus. He told her of his ultimate plan to return to the night of Holly's death and prevent its occurrence, and how his partners Steve, Fred and Patrick were going to send him back in time in longer increments each sojourn to make sure that he could make it back far enough to rescue her. Emily listened intently, and though the story Jack related was fantastical, she somehow knew it all to be true. They spoke for more than an hour, Emily probing for understanding and clarification at every opportunity. As they drove back to San Francisco, Emily spoke.

"I know that you don't want to do it, but I really think you need to talk to Dad about all of this," said Emily. "He may know something about all of this work. I'm pretty sure he still has some involvement with the CIA. Maybe he does have some insight as to your super genes."

"That's exactly what I was thinking," said Jack. "But I'm worried that he may try to stop me. Anyway, at this point I'm not sure that it really matters if he knows anything about my parents and the genes that they passed on to me." Jack paused a moment in thought. "Look, I'm sure I'll talk to him about it, but just not now. I want to get a little further down the road with all of this. So just don't say anything to anyone right yet, okay?"

"I won't. And you're sure that this Oberman guy is legit?" Emily asked.

"I trust those guys with my life," said Jack.

"Obviously!" Emily said.

10

Patrick had completed the design and modifications of Jack's etartenepon disguise and had fine-tuned the quantum targeting device. The team was ready to send Jack back in time in the first increment. Steve, Patrick, Fred and Jack were huddled around the flat-screen monitor, reviewing diagrams and time lines. Their task now was to determine exactly where and, more importantly, when, to send Jack.

"I've been giving some thought to that," said Jack. "I want to go here." He unfolded a section of the San Francisco Examiner and laid it upon the table. The article was a follow-up piece on the mysterious murder of the young woman in Golden Gate Park.

"I want to go back to this date and I want to save this girl," said Jack.

Steve was nonplussed. "Absolutely not, Jack," he said. "This is a trial run only. We're trying to make sure we can pull this off. We are running a test, there and back, real quick, nothing more."

"Listen," Jack pleaded his case. "You're going to send me back anyway. This fits into the frame of the time increment of how far you want me to go back on this first trial. Let's make some use of it. Let's do some good."

"That is such a bad idea on so many levels," Steve insisted. "We don't even know if this will work. You may not survive! We have all talked about the purpose of this first trial and it was not to save some Jane Doe!"

"Exactly!" Jack asserted. "I may not survive. I understand that and I'm willing to take the risk. But in exchange for taking that risk, I want some good to come of all this. I can save this girl!"

Steve picked the newspaper up from the table and read the article as he paced. Upon completion, he addressed his partners.

"Gentlemen, we don't know anything about this girl," he said. "We don't know anything about the circumstances of her death. Who is she? *What* is she? If Jack saves her, it is going to alter history. What will result? We don't know. We can't assume the risk."

"Everything about this is a risk," insisted Jack. "This was a girl who got mugged in a park. She was someone's daughter. She was probably a tourist. How could saving her cause a problem?"

Steve did not feel at all good about this. He did not like when his plans were changed; he did not like to relinquish control. Still, he felt the eyes of his partners upon him and sensed that they all wanted to save this girl. He knew that Jack had the final say. Only he could make the trip back in time, and Steve needed Jack to make that trip.

"Let's see what we can find out about her," said Steve.

Patrick knew Steve well enough to understand that he had just assented to Jack's proposed mission. He looked at Jack with a smile. "All right, Time Man, you really *are* going to be a superhero!" said Patrick.

Jack just shook his head. "Will you please stop with the superhero mantra?" he said.

While Patrick and Jack discussed and planned the specifics of his travel to Golden Gate Park at the chosen time, Fred and Steve researched the public record for information on the murder of the unknown girl in the park. They reassembled after supper and huddled around the worktable upon which Steve and Fred had spread various documents.

"These are all of the news reports surrounding the girl's murder." Steve indicated a pile of papers. "This is the police report," he said, indicating another stack, "and this is the coroner's report that Fred procured. The police report concludes that the girl was jogging in the park and was the victim of a mugging gone badly." Steve looked at Jack. "But there are inconsistencies," he said.

"How so?" asked Jack.

Fred interjected. "Look at the autopsy report," he said, holding up the file. "The coroner places the time of death at approximately 12:45 a.m. Why would she be jogging then? And there's more." Fred read from the report. "'The victim is a Caucasian female, 5 feet 4 inches tall weighing 120 pounds with shoulder length brown hair, wearing drawstring sweatpants and a long sleeve athletic shirt.'" Fred looked up. "She had no pockets. There's nothing to steal." He continued reading. "'Three gunshot wounds are noted. One lethal shot to the back of the head occurred ante mortem; a second wound to the chest and a third wound to the abdomen occurred post mortem. Additionally, multiple contusions to the head, face and arms occurred post mortem.'" Fred looked up again at Jack.

"What does all of that mean?" asked Jack.

Steve answered, "It means that the girl was executed by a single shot to the head. All of the other injuries were inflicted after she died to make it appear as if she was the victim of a mugging."

Jack considered for a moment. "If you guys figured this out, surely the police should have as well," he said.

"I'm sure that they did," said Steve. "There is something going on here that they are covering up for whatever reason. This girl was not mugged, she was targeted, and the police are hiding that fact."

Jack walked toward the window and peered out vacantly as he pondered. Clearly this girl was involved in something that was way over her head. But what was it? Why was she in the park at that hour and what was she doing? Why were the police covering up the true circumstances of her murder? Far from being dissuaded, Jack felt more compelled to save her and find the answers to those questions. He turned to his partners.

"I still want to go back and save her," he said. "I don't know what it is, but something deep inside tells me that is what we need to do."

Steve stared Jack in the eyes intently as though he was trying to gaze into his soul. Jack stared back without blinking. On some level, the two men were communicating. After what seemed to be an eternity, Steve spoke.

"Then let's construct a plan to get you there," he said.

Over the course of the next three days, the team did devise a plan. Steve, Patrick and Fred worked day and night. Jack joined them after his workday, having run the course of his two-week vacation. The four men now huddled around the flat-screen monitor to review their work. Patrick pulled up a satellite image on Google Maps.

"This is Golden Gate Park," said Steve. "The girl's body was found on the southwest bank of Metson Lake, here." He indicated the location. "But, that is not where she was killed. Her body was moved there in an attempt to delay its discovery." Steve looked at Jack. "Presumably she was killed nearby, but we don't know exactly where. We can get you in the vicinity, but you're going to have to find her."

Jack suddenly felt nauseated; this was becoming all too real. *Am I going to be able to pull this off?* he pondered.

Steve noticed his pallor. "You okay, Jack?"

Jack collected himself, pushing that seed of doubt from his mind. "Yeah, I'm fine. Go ahead," he said.

Steve continued, "Patrick will place the quantum targeting device here, behind the stables at the polo field. We'll get you there at 12:20 a.m." Steve looked somberly at Jack. "Remember, we can only keep the portal open for thirty minutes. That means you have to locate the girl, get her out of trouble and be back through the portal by 12:50 a.m. You understand that, right?"

Jack cocked his head dubiously. "That still doesn't seem like very much time," he said.

"It's not," said Steve. "But that's all you get. Are you sure that you want to go through with this?" he asked.

"Yeah, I'm sure," Jack responded without hesitation.

Steve pressed on. "If you haven't found her by 12:50 or if you can't prevent her murder by that time, you have to abort the mission. Do you understand?"

Jack nodded. "Yes, I understand."

Steve looked at Patrick and nodded, indicating that he was finished with the review. Patrick shut down the monitor.

"Okay, let's go reconnoiter," said Steve.

The team left the warehouse and headed to Golden Gate Park. Once they arrived, they studied every inch of the property, particularly the area where the girl's dead body was found. It was such a beautiful place for such an ugly crime. Jack was only hours away from returning to that scene at that time.

The next day, the team was hard at work making

final preparations. Jack left work early to join them and found Steve and Patrick working on Jack's time travel devices. Fred was off site, utilizing one of the medical center research labs to study Jack's latest test results. Patrick and Steve exchanged greetings with Jack upon his entry into the warehouse.

"Hey Jack. I'm just finishing up calibrations to sync the quantum polarizer, the quantum targeting device and the glasses," said Patrick. "Come give these a try," as he handed Jack the sunglasses of his disguise.

Jack put them on. "Wow! I wasn't expecting that!" said Jack. Though the lenses of the glasses were dark, Jack found his vision with them on to be exceptional.

"Pretty cool, huh?" said Patrick. "The quantum spectra lenses admit the optimal amount of light suited to your retinas. So whether it's dark, light, bright or overcast, you will see as though the lighting is perfect."

Jack scanned the warehouse and was amazed at the clarity.

"There's more," Patrick continued. "A microprocessor in the arm of the glasses will register and react to any change in the lens of your eye. When your lenses accommodate to see near or far, the glasses will accentuate that action. That means you can see twice as far as you naturally would, and have near microscopic vision up close."

Jack picked out a spot on the far wall and looked at it. As he concentrated on it, the spot magnified and came into sharp focus. "Amazing," was all that he could say.

"Now put in the earbud," Patrick directed.

Jack placed the form-fitted earpiece dangling from the arm of the glasses into his ear.

"It works the same way for hearing," said Patrick. "Just concentrate upon what you want to hear, and the processor will amplify that sound and cut out all the competing background noise and distortion."

Jack looked toward the sink at a slow dripping of water. He concentrated upon that drip, bringing it sharply into acoustic focus until the sound of dripping was all that he heard. *Amazing!* he thought. Jack removed the glasses and turned to Steve.

"How in the world does this work?" he asked.

"Think of it as a Wi-Fi network linked to your brain," said Steve. "Each device is configured to your molecular makeup. The glasses are synced with your lenses and retinas; the earpiece is synced with your eardrum and cochlea. They are in essence an extension of your optic and acoustic nerves, respectively. They are an upgrade of your senses of sight and hearing."

"Unbelievable," said Jack. What he really found to be unbelievable was that he understood the concept.

"You should wear the glasses and earpiece to acclimate to them," said Patrick. "The more you wear them, the better you'll be able to control them."

Jack compliantly donned the glasses and inserted the earbud. He walked to the mirror to inspect his appearance. "These look better than my Wayfarers," he said.

Steve picked up the wrist-worn quantum polarizer and handed it to Jack. "Put this on too," he instructed.

"This looks sharp! And it tells time," he said as he admired the device. "It's deceptively lightweight," he noted.

Patrick gloated, "It's made of a derivative of etartenepon; not quite as strong but better suited for radioactive devices."

Jack's head shot up. "Radioactive?" he asked with concern.

"Don't worry, it is perfectly sealed and contained."

Jack looked dubiously at Patrick, but Patrick didn't notice. Jack inspected the device closely and noted not only the knob that activated the polarizer, but also a knob opposite the first that had not been on the prototype. "What does this one do?" he asked.

"That one has not been activated; we'll go over that later," Steve said dismissively.

Jack was so overwhelmed with all of the technology that he was wearing that Steve's answer appeased him for the moment.

"Are you ready to give it a try?" asked Steve.

"Let's do it," Jack replied.

With Patrick carrying the targeting device, they walked over to what was now the molecular exchange pod. The device had been modified so that instead of a small cage, a large glass pod existed that could accommodate a grown man. Ultimately, Jack would enter and molecular exchange would occur within that glass pod. Unlike the previous system, the pod was completely sealed, averting the risk of a containment breach of the beam. Steve reviewed the process with Jack:

"Without the targeting device, if the molecular exchange pod is activated with you inside of it, you will be sent back in time and will later rematerialize back in the molecular exchange pod after the amount of time you were sent back has lapsed. The targeting device allows us to transport you to another location. When the targeting device is configured to the pod and synced to you, the portal will open wherever the targeting device is placed. The portal will stay open in that location for thirty minutes. In order for you to access the portal, you must polarize the molecular vibration of the portal to match your molecular vibration, which you will do by activating the polarizing device."

Steve indicated the wristwatch that Jack was wearing. "Your glasses will then allow you to see the portal," he continued. "It will appear as a curtain of blue flowing mist." Steve turned his attention to Patrick. "Place the targeting device over there," he said, indicating a location halfway across the warehouse.

Patrick placed the device on the floor at the designated location and activated it. Steve gave a nod of affirmation and closed the door to the molecular exchange pod.

"One more thing," said Steve, again addressing Jack. "Remember that in order to match the vibratory polarity of the portal to yours, you are going to have to be within fifty feet of it. You're going to have to know its location within at least that distance in order to find it when you activate the polarizer."

With the pod door now closed, Steve walked over to the control console and activated the molecular exchange beam. The pod filled with a blue shimmering mist of energy.

"Look over there," he said to Jack, pointing to the targeting device. "Can you see the portal?" he asked.

"No, nothing," Jack replied.

"Patrick, stand behind the targeting device," instructed Steve. Patrick rounded the device and stood behind it. "Look closer, Jack. Can you see what looks like a heat shimmer?"

"Yeah, it looks like a mirage on the highway on a hot summer day."

"Now, activate the polarizer," instructed Steve.

Jack depressed the activation knob of the polarizing device. Immediately he saw the same blue shimmering curtain of energy as was present in the molecular exchange pod. He could not see Patrick standing behind it.

"Do you see it now?" Steve asked.

"Yes I see it, plain as day," said Jack.

"That is what you are going to pass through to get back here in real time," said Steve. "Remember, Jack, if you're not within fifty feet, you won't see it. That's very important."

"I understand," Jack nodded.

Jack depressed the knob again and the portal vanished

from view. Steve shut down the beam of the molecular exchange pod. "One more thing, and then we'll stop for the day," he said. "Patrick has your disguise ready."

"Let's suit you up, Time Travel Man," said Patrick teasingly.

Jack shook his head as he followed Patrick into the makeshift dressing room to change into the etartenepon suit. Patrick pulled the various components of the disguise together and laid them out for Jack.

"Okay, Destiny Man, put on the bodysuit," said Patrick.

Jack stripped down to his boxer briefs and worked his way into the etartenepon bodysuit. Patrick handed him the pullover shirt and the black Special Forces pants, then Jack worked his way into the boots. Patrick helped him with the duster topcoat, after which Jack donned the beret and glasses and set in the earpiece. The ensemble was complete.

Patrick once again went over every protective feature and asset of the suit. He explained again how the bodysuit was impenetrable to knives, bullets and any other penetrating weapon or projectile. He and Jack worked for hours until Jack mastered the suit's features and had an almost reflexive control of them. Jack was ready. He and his team had reconnoitered the park; Patrick would set the targeting device behind the stables, and tomorrow Jack would travel back in time to save a girl he didn't even know.

What he did know was that somebody loved that girl

and wanted her back. He knew that feeling. *It's hell to lose someone you love*, he thought. Yes, Jack was ready; he was ready to take the first step in his quest to reunite with Holly.

11

"You're still hesitant about me saving the girl, aren't you?" Jack asked Steve.

The two men sat drinking morning coffee while Patrick and Fred finalized the sequencing of the molecular exchange pod. Jack knew that Steve had reservations; he had them too.

"There are just so many unpredictable eventualities," said Steve. "Not the least of which is that no one has ever done this before, at least as far as we know. All that we have to go by is one accidental time transport that was totally fortuitous, and books full of theories and formulas. Throw on top of that the fact that you are going to attempt to save the life of some unknown girl under very dangerous circumstances, and that we have no idea what the result will be if you are successful; yeah, I'm a little hesitant."

Jack was not comforted by Steve's comments, but he

was determined to forge ahead. He was willing to risk his life to get back to Holly, and this was the first step.

"Think of all the scientific discoveries and advancements that came about by way of serendipity," Jack said. "I believe that there is a greater force that guides humanity and individuals when we are too stupid or too slow to figure it out on our own. I don't believe those things are accidental; I believe that they result from Divine intervention." Jack paused a moment. "We weren't brought together by accident, but rather by design. And though I don't know why, I also believe that part of that design is to save the girl."

"I hope that you're right," said Steve, staring ahead vacantly in thought as he sipped his coffee. Jack made certain not to disrupt his contemplation. After a few moments Steve spoke again.

"Jack, you have to be disciplined when you travel back in time," he said. "You are likely to come across many circumstances that you are going to want to change, for example the murder of this girl. Your dilemma is going be to determine which of those things you have to leave unaltered. All of the time-space continuum theorists posit that an alteration of a single event in history can have exponential repercussions for the present and future. We can't predict what those repercussions will be. You are going to have to decide if you are going to trade a history that you know, whether it be good or bad, for one that you don't know. That is an awesome responsibility."

"The whole reason I'm doing this is to change history," said Jack. "Holly's death was an aberration of history; it should not have occurred."

"I know, Jack; I understand that."

"Do you think it is wrong for me to save the girl in the park?"

"Of course it's not wrong; she was murdered after all. Is it what you should do? I can't answer that," said Steve. He paused and took another sip of coffee. "You say that you feel compelled to save her. I can't argue with that. Maybe there is a powerful force guiding you, Divine Providence, God, the Universe, whatever you call it. Maybe that is going to be your best guide. Whatever it is, it's likely to be your only guide. You'll have to rely upon it; it's all that you'll have."

"I understand your concerns," acknowledged Jack. "I know that I can't change everything. Nor do I feel a compulsion to do so. But I do know that I have to go back for Holly, and I do know that for whatever reason I have to save the girl in the park. Those are wrongs that need to be righted, and I can do that."

Steve looked Jack squarely in the eyes, searching his soul once again. "I trust you, Jack. For some reason there is no one I trust more with the fate of history than you." Steve lifted his coffee mug. "Here's to you, Yesterman."

"Yesterman," Jack repeated. "Hmm, I like that," he said as he raised his mug to Steve.

Patrick and Fred walked over. "Everything is set," said Fred. "Are you ready, Jack?"

"I'm ready."

"Let's get you suited up, Yesterman," said Patrick with an impish grin, having overheard the moniker. Jack smiled in return.

Jack emerged from the back room, dressed in his disguise. He was calm, he was confident, he was prepared, he was equipped, and he was Yesterman. Steve on the other hand was not so well poised. He was as anxious as a person could be as he tinkered with controls at the console. When he saw Jack, he stood and approached him. "Do you have any questions? Is there anything about the plan or equipment with which you are not comfortable?" he asked nervously.

"I know how everything works; I've studied the park; I know where the targeting device will be and where to find the portal. I know the timeline; I know I have only thirty minutes. I'm ready," Jack said.

Steve's apprehension was not allayed. "Where are the glasses?" he asked Jack in a panic.

Jack pulled them from his inner coat pocket and put them on his face. "You look like you're about to be married," Jack observed teasingly. "Calm down, we're ready," he assured Steve.

Steve gave a nervous laugh. "You're right, we are ready. Patrick and I must have run systems checks at least five times," he said. Patrick rolled his eyes behind Steve's back.

"I'll be communicating with you throughout the mission," said Steve. "As long as the portal remains open we can speak to each other. Once the portal closes we're done, so be back by 12:50."

"Got it," Jack acknowledged.

"I'll be monitoring your vital signs, oxygen consumption and neurological parameters," said Fred. "I'll notify you if anything is awry. If I tell you to come back, do so, no questions asked."

"I understand," said Jack.

"I'll be keeping up with your location, both in time and space," said Patrick.

"One more thing," said Steve. "Take this and secure it." He handed Jack a flash drive. "This drive contains all of our data pertaining to the molecular exchange pod. If for some reason we can't get you back, find me in the past and give it to me."

"I'm going to make it back," Jack said.

"I know, I know. Take it just in case."

Jack tucked the drive into one of his pant pockets and zipped the pocket closed. Steve stepped back and surveyed the scene. There was nothing more to do. "Okay, let's go," he said.

Jack walked into the molecular exchange pod and held fast to the handrails for support as Steve closed and latched the door. Patrick and Fred went to their respective monitoring stations and Steve sat at the console. He put on a headset and addressed Jack.

"How are you doing in there?" he asked.

"I'm good," replied Jack, sounding anything but.

"Okay Jack, hold tight, just a couple of final checks,"

said Steve. He then addressed Patrick. "Targeting device?"

Patrick accessed the GPS signal from the targeting device and noted it to be exactly where he had placed it earlier. "Targeting device in place and active," he said.

Steve turned to Fred. "Fred?"

Fred analyzed the monitors displaying all of Jack's vital functions. "All good," he said. Steve gave Fred a nod.

"Okay. Ready, Jack?" asked Steve.

"Ready," Jack replied.

"Hold on tightly," advised Steve. "You're going to feel off balance for a bit."

Jack took a deep breath and steadied his stance, holding tightly to the handrails. He was scared to death. He kept his thoughts on Holly. Steve adjusted the controls as he gave one last check to the system. "Off you go, Yesterman," he said, as he activated the molecular exchange pod with a silent fervent prayer.

The hum from the exchange pod gradually became louder, as Jack was surrounded by a blue shimmering mist that ultimately obscured him from sight within the pod. As the humming diminished, so did the blue hue. When it cleared, the pod was empty.

***

Jack heard the hum of the exchange pod and felt a strong static thrumming before a blue electrically charged cloud, replete with lightning flashes, enveloped him. The hum turned to the sound of rushing wind, as if from a tornado. In fact Jack felt as though he was caught in a tornado, being spun around by a terrific centrifugal force. That force was becoming unbearable. Jack clinched his eyes closed and reflexively executed the Valsalva maneuver to prevent blood from rushing out of his brain, not registering the fact that at that moment his brain was a conflagration of scattered molecules. He felt on the verge of passing out as he stifled a disembodied scream. Suddenly the vortex stopped. Jack opened his eyes and saw in front of him the now familiar blue curtain. After taking but a moment to compose himself, he stepped through the curtain and into the Golden Gate Park of the past. He checked his watch. The time was 11:20 p.m.

Jack found himself immersed in total darkness. But no sooner did that register than his glasses made the instantaneous adjustments to optimize his vision. Jack saw that he was behind the polo stables exactly as planned. As he turned to look behind him, the curtain of the portal faded and disappeared. Jack made mental note of its location, then walked toward the previously designated observation point.

"Jack, can you hear me?" Steve's voice momentarily startled Jack.

"Yes, I hear you."

"Fred says you had quite a journey but all of your physiologic parameters have normalized. How do you feel?"

"I'm fine, a little dizzy at first but that has resolved. It wasn't a bad trip," Jack lied.

"Patrick is tracking your location. All systems go," said Steve.

Jack acknowledged as he continued to covertly skirt around the polo field. At the southwest curve of the field he came upon his observation point: a utility box positioned behind a row of hedges. Jack climbed atop it and peered through the hedges. He scanned the area utilizing the telescopic enhancement of his glasses. His eye caught motion along the drive by the softball field in the distance. He brought the image into magnified focus and saw a girl walking along the path. He zoomed in to the image and saw that she was wearing sweatpants and a long-sleeved athletic shirt. This was the girl.

"Got her," Jack said.

"Careful, Jack," Steve replied.

Jack focused acoustically until he could hear her footsteps crunching the gravel beneath her shoes. From across the road that ran alongside the polo field, Jack registered voices coming from behind a line of trees that bordered a lake. He focused his sight in that direction but could obtain no visual of the origin of the voices. But he thought that he had heard one of the voices somewhere before.

"There she is, right on time," said the disembodied voice.

Jack turned back to the girl, who continued to make her way toward his position. She stopped at the southeast curve of the polo field and appeared to be waiting. Jack turned his attention back across the road toward the lake as he heard the sound of motion. Three men in dark clothing emerged through the trees at the northeast shore. Jack brought the men into sharp focus, and recognized the same thugs led by the skinhead who attacked Cho at the market. Jack was puzzled. *What are they doing here?* he wondered.

"I see them, northeast shore of the lake," relayed Jack.

The thugs move slowly but deliberately toward the girl. As they crossed the road between the lake and the polo field, two of them fell back, presumably to serve as lookouts. The skinhead continued toward the girl. As he came near, she spoke.

"You said that you would be alone," she said.

"Security. You wouldn't want us to be disturbed, would you?" questioned the skinhead.

"I don't like this; forget it," said the girl.

As she turned to walk away, the skinhead grabbed her and spun her around. Jack was poised to pounce when suddenly the girl delivered a blow to the skinhead's face, causing him to reel. Jack froze.

"Get your hands off me, punk," said the girl.

The skinhead raised his hands. "Okay, okay, don't freak out on me," he said. "Now come on, we can still do business."

Jack watched as she considered bolting, but the other two thugs were already upon her. She stayed put.

"Do you have the goods?" asked the skinhead.

"I can get it."

"The deal was that you would have it with you!"

"First, I want to know who is going to get it. I know you punks don't have that kind of money," she retorted.

"That wasn't the deal," said the skinhead.

"Well, it's part of the deal now," said the girl.

The skinhead was fuming. He nodded toward one of his companions, who in turn rounded the girl, grabbed her by her hair and twisted her arm behind her back, forcing her to her knees. Jack saw her grimace in pain. He jumped down from the utility box and began to move, when he heard Steve's voice.

"Fifteen minutes, Jack."

Jack did not reply. He edged along the rail of the polo field en route toward the girl and the thugs.

"Why do you want to know who we work for?" asked the skinhead suspiciously.

The girl replied through her pain, "I like to know who I'm doing business with."

The skinhead eyed her skeptically as he leaned over and moved his face up to hers. "I don't think so," he said. "I think you're a cop." He stared her down for a moment longer. "Our business is done," he said. The skinhead stood and walked behind the girl. His partner released the girl's hair as the skinhead raised a handgun and pushed the barrel against the back of her head.

In a flash Jack was upon them. His sudden appearance out of nowhere startled the skinhead; he turned and began firing his gun wildly in Jack's direction. The bullets that Jack didn't manage to dodge bounced off of his disguise. In seconds, Jack disarmed the skinhead and knocked him out cold. After what seemed to be an eternity of hesitation, the other two men lunged toward Jack. One attempted to plunge a knife into him but only succeeded in breaking off the blade. The etartenepon functioned well. Jack rolled him over his shoulder and into the third man. Having disabled them, he lashed their wrists together behind their backs with cable ties that he retrieved from his coat.

"Five minutes, Jack, time to go," Steve said.

"I copy," replied Jack. He wasn't even winded.

Jack bound the three men together as they started to rouse. The skinhead addressed him. "What the hell are you?" he asked.

Jack ignored the question. "Not such a tough guy now, are you?"

The girl was crumpled against the rail of the polo field, watching them in disbelief.

"Three minutes, Jack. You have to come now," said Steve with panic in his voice.

Jack rushed over to the girl. "Are you okay?"

"Who are you?"

"Get out of here now. Call the police and tell them where these guys are," was Jack's only response.

"Damn it, Jack, you have one minute! Move!" Steve was going to pieces.

Jack bolted. He jumped the rail of the polo field and raced toward the stables. The alarm on his watch was sounding; he had only five seconds to access the portal. Jack hurdled the opposite rail of the polo field and rounded the stable. As he did so, he activated the polarizer and the portal curtain came into view. His alarm sounded a steady tone indicting that time had expired, just as he leapt through the portal and disappeared from Golden Gate Park with a crack of lightning.

***

Steve, Patrick and Fred had their eyes glued to the molecular exchange pod. Patrick had tracked Jack to the portal, but couldn't be sure that he made it before the portal had collapsed. The pod was filled with the familiar blue electrical cloud. The men strained to see into the obscurity. As the molecular exchange pod powered down, the cloud began to fade. Yesterman's silhouette began to form. Patrick dropped his head and let out a sigh of relief. Fred remained intent upon Jack's vital signs and physiologic readings. Steve stood and walked over to the pod. When the cloud cleared he saw Jack holding to the handrails with his eyes closed. When Jack opened his eyes, he saw Steve's face and smiled. With trembling hands, Steve unlatched the door to the pod and assisted Jack out.

"We did it, she's safe," said Jack.

Steve squeezed Jack's shoulders and nodded affirmation, too overcome with emotion to speak.

"Well done, Yesterman," said Patrick.

Fred shut down his station and walked over to Jack. "Come on, let's check you out," he instructed.

12

Fred and Jack spent half the day testing, monitoring and running laboratory analysis. Jack checked out well. Once again Fred noted that Jack had become stronger and healthier as a result of the time transport. During that same time period Patrick returned to Golden Gate Park to retrieve the targeting device, ran system checks on all of the equipment and inspected Jack's disguise; Steve journaled the mission and perused news and police reports from the day. By midafternoon, the team assembled for a post-mission conference.

"You almost didn't make it back," said Steve.

"There's just not enough time. Is there any way to keep the portal open longer?" Jack said.

"It was starting to disrupt at thirty minutes," said Patrick. "That is the limit, but I'll keep working on it."

Jack gave the team a detailed recounting of his adventure, both the sensations he perceived during time travel and the events of the rescue. He also revealed that the thugs were the same men who had attacked Cho in the market. When Jack mentioned that, it occurred to him that Cho had thought those thugs were looking for him that day. *Could they have been looking for me?* he questioned himself.

Jack did not share that fact with the group, though. Steve documented everything that Jack said. Patrick then reviewed the GPS data and equipment logs. Everything had worked as planned and he saw no need for modifications. Fred reviewed the results of Jack's post-mission testing, and declared Jack fit and free of adverse sequelae. Steve reviewed with the team the information that he procured regarding the quantum physics of the project. He then launched into the news reports from the day, pulling his references up on the flat-screen monitor.

"These are reports from the morning after your rescue of the girl," he said. "Neither in newspapers nor in police reports is there any mention of a murder in the park. You did it."

Patrick patted Jack on the back.

"What about a police report on the arrest of the attackers?" Jack asked.

Steve scanned the police reports from that night and the few days after. "There's no report of any arrest. In fact, there are no reports of any occurrences in the park that night."

"I told her to call the police to have them arrested...

Why did she not do that?" Jack wondered. "Those thugs thought that she was a cop. Surely if she was she would have called it in."

"Did you get her name? I can pull up the police personnel records for San Francisco and the surrounding areas," said Steve.

"No, I don't know her name," said Jack. "Maybe she's some sort of federal agent."

"If she is, she likely wouldn't have used her real name anyway," said Steve. He dug further into the Internet files. "I can't find any information whatsoever on the girl or her attackers. If she is a cop or federal agent, they've locked this incident down."

"Those guys were the same ones that attacked Cho," Jack repeated. "How are they connected to this mystery girl? Clearly they thought that she was working undercover. There's got to be something there."

"Obviously they were threatened enough by her to want to kill her. What was she selling them?" Steve asked.

"I don't know, but she made it sound as though it was very expensive."

"I hope this wasn't a mistake, Jack," said Steve.

***

Max Dawson was sitting in his home study, intently poring over old files pertaining to Jack's parents that he had resurrected and laid out upon his desk. His face wore an expression of consternation, as the information activated synapses that had been long dormant. He had been studying the documents for hours when Sarah interrupted. Max looked up from his work at the sound of the opening door. "Hey baby," he said.

"Someone is here to see you."

As Sarah opened the door wider, Max noticed a young female guest. He stood and walked around the desk to greet her.

"Mr. Dawson, I'm Special Agent Suzanne Granger, FBI," she said as she presented her badge. "I need to speak with you about your son."

***

The skinhead who attacked Cho was sitting behind a glass partition in the visitor's area of the San Francisco Sheriff's Department County Jail. Andrei Gorski entered and sat opposite him on the other side of the partition. The skinhead twitched nervously as Gorski picked up the hand-held receiver that hung on the wall. The skinhead picked up the receiver on his side.

"I should not be here with you. What is so important?" Gorski asked tersely.

"The guy from the park in the crazy costume: he was Jack Dawson," said the skinhead.

"Why do you think that?"

"It was something he said. He said the same thing to me at the market. The voice was the same."

"What did he say?"

The skinhead was embarrassed. "He told me that I wasn't such a tough guy."

Gorski stared the man down. "You are pathetic. Jack Dawson humiliated you in the park, allowing the girl to escape. Then you can't manage to kill him when he practically offers himself to you on a platter at the market. You have caused me to lose all credibility with my superiors," said Gorski as he stood. "You will speak of this to no one, do you understand?"

"Yes, I understand," said the skinhead sullenly.

Gorski left, determined to be rid of Jack Dawson.

***

Jack spent the next couple of weeks at Hughes Investments during the day and with the Yesterman team during the evening hours. The next time travel increment was determined. One more interval before Jack could go back far enough in time to save Holly. He was becoming impatient and tried to convince the team to skip that next increment, but received no support.

So Jack scanned police and news reports to find another person he could help in the interim time increment, before he went back to Holly. Steve was still unsettled that he could find no information about the rescue of the mysterious girl who was attacked in the park. He was comforted, however, that no adverse repercussions appeared to result. When Jack presented what he wanted to do for his next mission, Steve's comfort evaporated. He read the articles that Jack brought him pertaining to the proposal.

"Jack, this is not a good idea," said Steve.

"Why not? It's perfect," said Jack.

"I don't think you can change this. This isn't an aberration of history. It is an intentional act," Steve said. "This could greatly alter universal order, and we have talked about not doing that."

"We also talked about a higher order that compels me. I feel compelled to do this."

"I'm afraid that I agree with Steve on this one," Fred offered. "You have no experience in dealing with something like this. It is a very complex situation and I don't think you can pull it off in thirty minutes, regardless of the impact on universal order. And thirty minutes is all that you have."

"You barely made it back last time," said Patrick. "If you try this and don't make it back, you'll lose your opportunity to go back to Holly."

"There has to be a way to work around the thirty-minute window," said Jack. "We need to do this. If we work out the logistics, will you support this mission?"

Steve considered, and knowing Jack's determination and intuition, felt he had no hard arguments against it if the time limitation could be overcome. He looked at Fred and Patrick and registered that they were waiting for his guidance.

"Patrick, if you can find a way to overcome the time

limit and Fred, if you can counsel Jack on how to pull this off, we have an airtight plan, then we'll consider it," said Steve, feeling the odds of all that occurring were small.

Steve's cell phone rang. "You guys get to work," he said as he rose to take the call.

Jack and the others started into the project. Ten minutes into their discussion Steve walked over, having completed his call. He stood over them and appeared terribly concerned.

He addressed Jack. "That was my father," he said. "He wants us to go to his house this evening."

"Your father? Why, what's up?" asked Jack.

"He said that he couldn't go into details over the phone, but he thinks you're in danger," Steve said.

"Me? What kind of danger?"

"Somebody wants you dead."

***

Emily was in her gallery escorting a very handsome man through the exhibit. He was tall and olive-complexioned, with dark wavy hair and sea-blue eyes, dressed in an elegantly tailored grey suit. She was mesmerized by his accent. He was so knowledgeable about art and they had spent half the day in engaged conversation. Now they sat in a secluded corner of the gallery under dim lights, sipping wine.

"Your art collection is beautiful, particularly your

work," said Nicolai. "But nothing in here is nearly as beautiful as you. Tell me about yourself and your family."

Emily told him of her parents, Max and Sarah, and of her brother Jack.

"What do your parents do?" asked Nicolai.

"Mainly they travel," said Emily. "They're retired."

"From what did they retire?" asked Nicolai, already knowing the answer.

"My mom was an off and on school teacher," said Emily. "Dad was with the government, you know, a civil servant."

Emily knew well enough to be vague when discussing her father's work. And Nicolai knew that she was being vague. He knew that Max Dawson was a onetime CIA operative. He was beginning to feel that Emily would not easily divulge her family secrets and that more drastic measures might be required. Yet, he pressed on.

"And what about your brother Jack, what does he do?"

"He works for an investment bank," said Emily. "He's pretty boring actually."

Nicolai knew that Jack was anything but boring. He had been apprised of Jack's dramatic involvement in the Asian market fiasco, and of his dramatic rescue of the old lady in Chinatown. Emily had not shared that. Nor did Emily mention that Jack was adopted, which Nicolai also knew to be true. Yes, Emily was not one to divulge information in casual conversation. Nicolai decided to go to Plan B. For a brief moment he felt badly for the girl. The moment passed quickly. After all, he was a professional killer.

"How would you like to join me for dinner this evening?" Nicolai asked. "I was planning to go to Katia's for a taste of home. If we leave now, I'm sure that I can get us a table."

"Sure, that sounds fun," said Emily. "I've never eaten there before."

"That is wonderful," said Nicolai. He stood and offered his hand. "Shall we?"

"Let's," said Emily. "Give me just one moment to tell my staff I'm leaving."

After checking out with her staff, Emily was escorted by Nicolai to his car. The two made the short drive to Fifth Avenue and parked along the street. They walked a block to Katia's, and saw that even at this early hour there was a crowd waiting outside the door.

"This is a popular place," observed Emily.

"Let me see what I can do," said Nicolai.

They made their way through the crowd and into the restaurant, where they were greeted by the host. "Table for two?"

"Yes, please," said Nicolai.

"Very good sir, and do you have a reservation?" asked the host as he looked at his reservation book.

"No, I am afraid not," said Nicolai.

"No problem, sir. I'm sure we can get you seated," said the host. He consulted his reservation book again. "It looks like the wait will be about an hour."

Nicolai leaned in and spoke to the host in Russian. After another casual glance at the reservation book, the host addressed Nicolai. "I believe your table is ready. Right this way, please."

Nicolai and Emily were escorted to a table and seated. Emily was impressed.

"What did you tell him to get this table?" Emily asked.

Nicolai smiled. "It turns out that we have a mutual friend," he said. That mutual friend was Andrei Gorski, only he wasn't really either man's friend.

Emily looked over the menu, and having never had Russian food before deferred to Nicolai to order, which he did. The waiter brought the zakuski tasting platter and a bottle of Abrau-Dyurso. This was followed by gol-ubtsi, a spicy mix of baked ground beef, onions and rice wrapped in cabbage leaves. Emily and Nicolai wined and dined and conversed. They had a lovely meal. In lieu of dessert, the couple decided to go to the nearby Inovino wine bar before returning to the gallery and Emily's car.

Nicolai pulled up to the bar and parked. He walked around the car to help Emily out and escorted her in. They found a secluded seating area and settled upon a sofa. As Nicolai ordered two glasses of wine, Emily excused herself to the lady's room. Nicolai used the opportunity of her absence to retrieve a small casing from his inner coat pocket and sprinkle its contents into Emily's wine glass. By the time Emily returned, her wine was sufficiently adulterated. It didn't take long for Emily to feel the effects.

"Oh my," she said. "I'm feeling a bit tipsy."

That was the last thing Emily remembered. When she came to, she found herself bedded in an elegant room under lush linens. Her head was pounding. *Oh no, what did I do?* Emily racked her brain, trying to remember the evening. She pulled down her covers and saw that she was completely dressed. *Thank God!* she thought.

She swung her feet over the edge of the bed and sat up. It felt like her head was going to explode. She looked around the room and saw her purse on a nearby dresser. She walked unsteadily toward it and checked its contents. Everything was there; everything except for her cell phone.

Emily opened the bedroom door and walked down a long hallway. She heard the voices of two men speaking a foreign language. She emerged into an elegant great room where she spied Nicolai and another man. As she walked in, the two men took note of her.

"Ah, there she is now," said Nicolai. "Emily, I would like to present to you Andrei Gorski."

Gorski stood to greet her. In his hand was her cell phone.

13

The estate of Steven Oberman, Sr. was as ostentatious as it was massive. Situated overlooking the bay in Belvedere, it was a 45-minute drive from the historic district of San Francisco. Steve parked in the large circular drive at the front of the house. The team emerged from his Subaru and entered the house through its massive front door and traversed the elegant marble-floored entryway, past a spiral staircase to the back of the home.

Steve opened the huge mahogany double doors leading into his father's study. He, Jack, Fred and Patrick entered to find Steve Oberman, Sr. standing in front of a large fireplace, deep in conversation with another man. Oberman was a distinguished looking yet somewhat overweight man, impeccably dressed. He and the other man turned to regard the group. Jack was startled, recognizing Oberman's guest.

"Dad?" queried Jack confusedly.

"Hello, son," said Max Dawson.

Oberman went over to Jack and extended his hand. "Hello, Jack, I'm Steven Oberman." Jack shook his hand as Steve questioned his father.

"What's going on?" Steve asked.

"How 'bout we let this young lady get you boys up to speed," Oberman said, as he directed them to the heretofore unnoticed visitor standing by the bookcases.

Jack recognized her immediately as she walked toward them. She was the mystery girl from Golden Gate Park.

"Hello, gentlemen, I am Special Agent Suzanne Granger, FBI." She presented her badge with her introduction. "I suggest that we all sit; this is going to be a bit convoluted," she said.

Oberman escorted the group to a large round conference table situated left of the door at the front of the study. He invited everyone to sit and Suzanne launched right in.

"For the past eighteen months I have been investigating the activities of the Obshina operating in the United States." She registered the confusion upon the faces of her audience. "The Obshina is the Chechen Mafia. It is an organization that has radical Islamic leanings and as such has been on our radar for some time. The group had been relatively quiescent until about nine months ago." She turned to Jack. "That is when the cell in San Francisco acted on information that they learned about you."

"They acted on information about me? What kind of information? Why would the Chechen Mafia be interested in me?" Jack asked.

"Do you remember a series of reports that a reporter named Megan Hart ran, regarding you and your wife when your wife was killed?" Suzanne asked.

"Yeah, I mean I never saw the reports but I heard about them," Jack said.

"Well, in the course of those reports Ms. Hart revealed a little-known fact about you."

"What fact?"

"The fact that you were the biological son of Jennifer and Ken MacKenzie," said Suzanne.

Jack looked at her quizzically.

Suzanne continued. "The section boss of the Obshina in the U.S. is Andrei Gorski. He happens to be based in San Francisco. Gorski was formerly an officer in the KGB before the breakup of the Soviet Union in 1991. He was intimately knowledgeable about the activities of your parents. Gorski picked up on that fact."

Jack turned to Max, obviously confused. "Dad, what activities, what is she talking about?"

Max Dawson drew a deep breath. The time had finally come. "Son, are you aware of the work Steven and his company have done in the service of our country?"

"Steve told me some of what they have done. What does that have to do with my mom and dad? What does that have to do with me?"

"You know that your father and mother were good friends of ours," said Max.

"Yeah, that's how I ended up with you two," said Jack.

"What you don't know, son, is that I worked with Jennifer and Ken," said Max. "In fact, I was their supervisor."

"You worked with them? But you were in the CIA."

"That's right, son, I was in the CIA. So were your parents, working under me."

"My mom and dad were CIA agents?" asked Jack incredulously.

"Ken and Jennifer were a team, son," said Max.

Jack was dumbfounded. *I thought dad was a banker and mom was a housewife.* So many questions ran through his mind. He could barely process this information. "Did they have a connection to Oberman Enterprises?"

Max looked to Steven Oberman. "They had a very intimate connection," Oberman said. "By the late 1960s, Oberman Enterprises had sequenced the entire human genome. We had mastered cloning and perfected the ability to insert any gene for any trait into any individual. Having worked with the CIA throughout the process of that research, they engaged us in a program to exploit the advantages of genetic enhancements for their agents. Your mom and dad volunteered to be the first team."

"In 1971 Jennifer and Ken had their entire genomes enhanced," said Max.

"What do you mean by enhanced?" Jack asked.

"Genes for every desirable trait; strength, vision,

speed, everything, was cloned and inserted into their DNA."

"Your parents took on the characteristics promulgated by those enhancements. In effect, they became super agents," said Oberman.

"Whoa!" blurted out Patrick. Steve shot a silencing glance his way.

"Jennifer and Ken operated all over the world under my supervision," Max continued. "That is until Jennifer became pregnant with you in late 1979. She retired from field duty at that time but continued to work with me in support of Ken. Your parents functioned as genetically enhanced agents from 1971 until their assassination by the KGB in 1985, when you were five years old. By that time it was already clear that you had inherited their genetic superiority."

"My parents were assassinated by the KGB?" asked Jack dazedly. "I thought they were killed because of a fuel leak."

"They were killed by a Soviet car bomb, son," said Max.

Jack was speechless. Fred, however, was not. The origin of Jack's genetic superiority was now quite clear. "How many other enhanced agents were there?" Fred asked.

"None," said Suzanne. "The program was slated to have an observation and study period of five years. Mr. Dawson was next in line to undergo enhancement, but soon after President Carter took office in 1977, he closed down the program and had it sealed. Nobody can tell me why. Only recently have the files been made available."

Jack's head was still swimming. Max continued. "When Jennifer and Ken were killed, Sarah and I took you in. We knew that you carried those enhanced genes and we knew that if the KGB suspected that, they would have you killed as well. So, false information was leaked that you too were killed in the explosion. We secretly adopted you, gave you our last name, and moved to San Francisco to raise you like any other kid," said Max. "We kept you off of their radar screen. I'm sorry for not telling you all of this before, son, but we were trying to protect you."

Jack sat frozen.

"You were off their radar until Megan Hart's stories aired," said Suzanne. "Those reports that identified your parents put you squarely in the middle of Andrei Gorski's sights. We believe that he had the resources to confirm that you were the son of Jennifer and Ken MacKenzie, and that you in fact had not been killed."

"How did Megan Hart know that Jennifer and Ken MacKenzie were my biological parents?" Jack asked.

"I don't know, son," said Max. "Apparently we didn't clean up the trail as well as we thought we had. When it came out, we hoped no one would take notice. Obviously we were wrong."

"We think that it was just a crazy coincidence that Gorski was the KGB agent who was working to neutralize your parents," said Suzanne coolly. "When he confirmed that you were in fact the son of Jennifer and Ken, he rounded up the gang that attacked you and your wife outside the art gallery. He told them that you were trying to find them and if you did, would turn them over to the police. He convinced them that you had good leads and were closing in on them. It was really very easy for Gorski to recruit them to kill you."

"How do you know all of this?" Jack asked.

"I infiltrated that group posing as a contract worker for the NSA, looking to sell secrets to the Obshina. They wanted me to help track you down and in exchange, they would get me a meeting with Gorski. Somehow I was made and three weeks ago I was nearly killed. Someone saved me but no one in the agency knows who it was, or how they knew I was there and in danger."

Jack looked her in the eyes. "That's why you didn't call the police," he observed.

"What?"

"I told you to call the police and make sure those thugs got locked up," said Jack. "You couldn't because you were working undercover for the FBI."

"That was you?" said Suzanne in amazement.

"She's the girl from the park?" asked Steve incredulously.

"Whoa!" said Patrick again.

That shocking fact now revealed, Oberman nodded to his son to give an explanation. Steve addressed Suzanne. "We have been working on a device that allows for travel back in time," Steve said. "We sent Jack back to that time in the park when you were attacked. He is the one that saved you."

Suzanne was flabbergasted. Over the course of the next hour, Steve and Patrick explained to Suzanne how it came to be that they developed the molecular exchange pod and how they discovered it to be a time travel machine. They described the nuances and the intricacies of its function. Though Oberman had briefed Max earlier on the development, he too was interested to learn the fine details. Fred explained the testing that he performed upon Jack and the astounding results, and Jack told of his experience in time travel, beginning with the day that he fell off the wrong side of the bed. Much of what Suzanne learned she had to accept on faith, having absolutely no basis in advanced quantum theorem. She was now informed as much as anyone could be by such a crash course.

"How did you know that I was going to be attacked?" she asked.

"Your murder was reported in the paper," said Jack.

Suzanne turned pale. "My murder?"

"Suffice it to say that because of my son and these young men, your murder never occurred," said Max.

"So you saved my life. Thank you," said Suzanne to Jack.

"It was nothing," said Jack modestly.

Having gotten over the shock of the truth about his parents, and confident that Suzanne was up to speed on the details of the molecular exchange pod, Jack directed the conversation back to the problem at hand. "So, I'm not in the CIA and the Cold War is over. Why does the Chechen Mafia care about me?"

"They presume that, like your parents, you are genetically enhanced. That makes you a threat," said Suzanne. "The Obshina deals with threats by eliminating them. I'm here to prevent that. Turnabout is fair play, I guess," she said with a smile.

"Then you think that they will come after me again?"

"They already have."

That got everyone's attention. She continued, "Did you not recognize the man who held the gun to my head?"

"Yeah, he was the guy who held up Cho at the market."

"Well, he is currently in jail for that crime," said Suzanne. "But that wasn't a robbery, Jack. That was a botched attempt to kill you."

"To kill *me*?"

"I interviewed Cho Nguyen," said Suzanne. "Those guys were looking specifically for you. They are the same men who attacked you outside the art gallery and killed your wife. They are the same thugs that Gorski recruited, by telling them that you were determined to find them and have them imprisoned."

Jack saw it all so clearly now. He remembered dismissing Cho when she said that they were looking for him at the time.

"And Gorski won't stop with that botched attempt,"

said Suzanne. "He has now brought in a professional assassin from Chechnya. Nicolai Popov is his name. We know he is in the States and presumably here in the Bay area, but we haven't located him as of yet."

"So if you know who they are, why don't you just move in and arrest them?" asked Jack.

"There are two problems," answered Suzanne. "First, I have been placed on administrative leave to 'recuperate.' That's shorthand for telling me that I've been taken off the case. Secondly, the incident in the park was significant enough that it was reported to the President. He was furious. He has ordered that all activity on your case be suspended. I'm not supposed to talk about this case, much less be here with you. Apparently the President believes that your death is acceptable collateral damage under the circumstances. I don't share that view."

"Special Agent Granger is here at the risk of losing her career in the FBI, possibly of being sent to prison," said Max. "This President is under the thumb of the Obshina and he is willing to sacrifice you to avoid provocation. He is relying on the Chechen Mafia to soften radical Islamic terrorism directed at our country and its citizens. I'm afraid that we are on our own."

Steve looked at Max Dawson. "Well sir, in my opinion we have the best team possible to take this matter head on," he said.

Jack now knew who the man was that raped and killed his wife. He was more determined than ever to go back and change that. "So what is our first move?" he asked.

"First we have to find Nicolai Popov," said Suzanne. "He is the immediate threat."

After a long discussion between Max and Suzanne as to how to go about accomplishing that task, Jack's phone rang. He pulled it from his pocket and looked to see who was calling.

"It's Emily," he said as he took the call. "Hey Em, can I call you back in a bit?"

The voice on the other end was not that of Emily. It was that of a male with a heavy Russian accent.

"Mr. Dawson, my name is Andrei Gorski. I have your sister."

14

The team was in Steven Oberman's study, huddled over papers, plots, maps and graphs with a sense of urgency. Andrei Gorski had Emily and had given Jack a deadline of forty-eight hours to trade himself for her. If he did not, she would be killed. Nicolai had obviously studied Jack well and informed Gorski of his greatest weakness. The Yesterman team, which now included Max, Suzanne Granger and Oberman, Sr., was in overdrive. Max and Suzanne agreed that a trade of Jack for Emily was out of the question. One never negotiates with terrorists and realizes a good outcome. The only option was to change the course of history so that Gorski never learned who Jack's biological parents were, thus avoiding the whole cascade of ensuing events, including Emily's kidnapping.

To that end, they had to prevent Holly's murder. In the hours following Gorski's phone call, Oberman, Sr.

had the molecular exchange pod and all of its supporting equipment and documents moved to his estate. In addition to an unimpeachable surveillance and monitoring system, he had armed guards posted around the perimeter of his property. His home's security thus made it the safest place for the equipment and for Jack. Oberman, Sr. knew that the government would in time discover the molecular exchange pod. His greatest concern, however, was to ensure that the Obshina did not get their hands on it first. In any event, they would have to complete their mission to alter history before anyone discovered the time travel machine, or Emily would be killed just as Holly had been. All would be lost. Steve was right though; they did have the best possible team to confront this situation head on, and with the molecular exchange pod they had time on their side.

Still, Steve was uncertain. He did not function well with time constraints and he had less than thirty-six hours to pull this off. But even before he could send Jack back to the point in time to prevent Holly from being murdered, he had to send him back in the next time increment. It was critical that Jack have that incremental jump to further strengthen him in preparation for the strenuous time travel that would ensue. Steve was not comfortable with the next incremental mission.

"I just don't like it, it's way too complex," he said.

"Technically, the plan is sound," said Patrick. "The only question really is whether or not Jack can endure the stress of multiple transports."

"I think he can, and those multiple jumps will further strengthen him for travel back to Holly," said Fred. "His last battery of tests showed that his strengthening continues with each jump."

"We need something simpler," insisted Steve.

"We don't have time to come up with another plan, Steve," said Jack urgently. "We have to be able to turn all of this around in less than thirty-six hours. That means I have to have one more incremental jump back in time before I can go back for Holly and stop all of this. We can do it. You just concentrate on finalizing the plan for the next jump."

Steve knew that Jack was right. They didn't have any more time. Though Jack was at risk in light of the rushed planning, Emily was in imminent danger of losing her life. There were no other good options. This plan had been in the works for a while and they had to go with it. Steve relented. "Okay, then you'll go tonight and by tomorrow I'll have you ready to go back for Holly."

He hoped that he was right. There was not much time, and a lot of room for error. Steve consulted the files and launched into the mission plans.

"Patrick, you take Suzanne and Mr. Dawson with you at 1:00 a.m. to set and activate the targeting devices," instructed Steve. "There will be less foot traffic then. They can keep an eye on them and collect them when the mission is complete. You hurry back here and we should be able to get Jack on his way by 2:00 a.m. at the latest."

Patrick nodded assent and headed off to brief Max and Suzanne.

"You guys finish up here, then Jack, you should rest," Steve said to Jack and Fred. "I'm going to work out the details of getting you back to Holly."

Steve gathered the loose documents back into the folder, closed it, and walked to his desk. Jack noted the caption on the folder and smiled.

Project Yesterman: Mission #2

The team worked on their respective tasks through the morning and into the night. Jack did lie down, but he did not rest well. His brief episodes of sleep were littered once again with disturbing dreams, anxiety and anticipation. The team assembled for their first meal around 10:00 p.m. They took the opportunity to review the mission, which was just hours away.

"Security will be posted at the time that we go to position the targeting devices," said Max. "Luckily I still have connections, so we will be unencumbered. They have been led to believe that I'm testing the feed from a communications satellite."

"That's great, Dad," said Jack.

"Mr. Dawson and I will stay with the devices until the mission is over and then bring them back here upon completion," said Suzanne.

"And once I have activated the devices and assure that

they are functioning properly, I'll head back here to monitor and track Jack," said Patrick.

"Jack, do you feel like you're ready? Can you do this?" Steve asked.

"I'm ready," said Jack confidently. "Fred has worked with me on how to approach the situation."

"Okay, then let's get ready," said Steve.

Jack, Fred and Patrick headed off to assemble and check all of the quantum traveling equipment and the physiologic monitoring system. Suzanne and Max accompanied them to collect the targeting devices when they were ready for deployment. Steve and his father worked on the next mission: to save Holly and thereby save Emily. Time was running short. At 12:45 a.m., Max, Suzanne and Patrick, targeting devices in hand, set off to the Golden Gate Bridge. As had been prearranged, they were readily granted access to the pedestrian path of the bridge, and by one o'clock the devices were positioned and activated. Patrick was back at the Oberman estate by 1:35 and assisted Jack into his disguise. At 1:50, Patrick, Fred and Steve were at their consoles running final checks. Shortly thereafter Jack, as Yesterman, accompanied by Oberman, Sr., entered the room.

"Everything is ready," said Steve to Jack.

"Let's roll," said Jack.

Jack entered the molecular exchange pod and took hold of the handrails. He wasn't looking forward to the sensations he was about to feel, especially multiple times. Oberman, Sr. latched the pod door and took up position next to Steve.

"Can you hear me, Jack?" asked Steve, checking the communication system.

"Yes, I hear you."

"Fred?"

"Good here," Fred replied.

"Patrick?"

"All systems go," said Patrick.

"Are you ready, Jack?"

"Ready."

"Godspeed, Yesterman," said Steve.

As he activated the molecular exchange pod it once again filled with blue mist. When the mist cleared, Yesterman was gone.

***

Yesterman emerged from the portal on the southeast side of the north tower of the Golden Gate Bridge, where one of the targeting devices had been placed. It was dark out and very little traffic was running at that early morning hour. After a moment, Yesterman's vision accommodated to optimize his sight, and he peered around the tower to see a young woman standing outside of the rail behind the tower, hidden from view. Yesterman heard her softly sobbing. He spoke just as the woman inched closer to the edge.

"Hello, Aimee," he said softly.

Startled, Aimee jumped back as she turned toward the voice. Yesterman saw that she was frightened.

"Don't be alarmed. I'm here to help you," he said.

Aimee strained her vision in an attempt to recognize the man who apparently knew her. "Who are you?" she asked.

"I'm a friend; someone sent to watch over you."

"Twenty-five minutes, Jack," Steve's voice came through the earpiece.

"I'm here to make sure that you get home safely tonight," said Yesterman.

Aimee turned back toward the water and moved closer to the edge of the bridge.

"I don't want to get home safely. Leave me alone, go away," she said through tears.

Yesterman moved toward her. "Stay away from me!" screamed Aimee.

He stepped back quickly. "Okay, I'm not moving. I'll stay right here," he said.

Yesterman and Aimee stood their ground in desperate silence for a moment.

"Aimee, this is not what Donavan would want for you. You do know that, don't you?" he asked.

Aimee was taken aback. She moved back toward the rail and faced Yesterman. "How do you know about Donavan? How do you know me? Who are you?" she asked in rapid succession.

"Twenty minutes," Steve's voice again floated through the earpiece.

"I'm someone who cares for you. I want you to be safe," said Yesterman.

Aimee began to cry in earnest. Yesterman stepped closer.

"I know that you are a dancer. I know that you are wonderfully talented. I know that Donavan was not only your teacher, but also your mentor. More importantly, Aimee, I know that Donavan was your one true love," he said.

Aimee brought her hands to her face and sobbed mightily into them.

Yesterman continued. "You have a beautiful and wonderful gift to offer this world. Donavan saw that in you. Your work here is not finished. You know that Donavan would think the same, don't you?" he asked. "I was sent here tonight so that you can finish the work to which God has called you."

Aimee unshielded her eyes and looked at Yesterman. "How do you know all of that? I don't even know who you are! How do you know what I'm called to do?" she asked angrily.

"Fifteen minutes, Jack," said Steve.

Yesterman was concerned that he was losing control of the situation. He knew that he had to act quickly. Out of nowhere a thought came to him.

"No, you don't know me. But I know you," said Yesterman. "Do you believe that you have a guardian angel?"

"I used to believe that, when I was a little girl," said Aimee.

"Believe it. I am your guardian angel," said Yesterman. "I have traveled a long way to be with you tonight to protect you."

"Almost time to go, Jack," said Steve.

"I don't believe you," said Aimee. "You don't much look like an angel."

"What do you think an angel should look like? A little fat baby with wings and a harp?" asked Yesterman.

Aimee chuckled through her tears at the image. "I don't know," she admitted.

"Your guardian angel looks like this," said Yesterman as he held out his arms in display. "Let's get down from here and get you home, okay?"

Aimee looked at Yesterman intently with tears still running down her face. "You don't know what Donavan meant to me. He was my world, my life," she said. "We were getting married. I don't want to go on without him. You just don't understand."

"Five minutes, Jack, come on!" Steve's voice was anxious. "You agreed not to do this again."

"I do understand," said Yesterman with sincerity. "I know what it is like to lose someone who is your life; to lose your solace, your refuge. I know the hurt and the emptiness and the despair. But I know too that you have to go on, as hard as it may be to do so."

"How can an angel lose someone?" asked Aimee skeptically.

"I wasn't always an angel. It was a long time ago," said Yesterman.

"Damn it Jack, two minutes. GO!" shouted Steve.

"Do you trust me?" Yesterman asked.

"I don't know," said Aimee.

"I want you to watch me. Don't take your eyes off me. Will you do that?" asked Yesterman.

Aimee nodded in affirmation. Yesterman activated the wrist polarizer and stepped backward. He disappeared in a flash right before Aimee's eyes. She stared at the emptiness in astonishment.

"Aimee," said Yesterman.

Aimee gasped and turned 180 degrees to see Yesterman again standing before her.

"Oh my God! Where did you… How did …" Aimee stammered.

"It's what angels do," said Yesterman. "Look, I know that Donavan was your everything. I know that from the time the two of you met at Julliard to the time you lost him, you envisioned sharing the rest of your life with him. I know that the love you have for him is so hard to find. I've been there. But I also know that that love did not die with Donavan. That kind of love is a bond that traverses space and time and circumstance. In some plane of existence Donavan is still with you, he still feels your love. He still has his love for you. It is that love that will give you the courage to go on. It will sustain you in a life that God is not ready for you to give up."

Aimee stepped back against the tower and slid down it to sit. She dropped her head and her tears dripped between her knees.

"Aimee, your life is a beautiful gift; a gift of heart, body and soul. It is a gift of talent that should be shared with all of humanity," Yesterman said. "Donavan shared the gift of his life with you. In him you saw the beauty that the world can offer. That gift from Donavan is carried on in you. His love is forever stamped on your heart and nestled within your soul. If you quit now, that gift will be lost. Complete Donavan's love, with your life."

Yesterman waited with Aimee in silence. She sobbed a bit longer, then dried her tears. She had made a decision. She looked to Yesterman. "I'm ready to go home," she said.

Yesterman reached out to Aimee, helped her to her feet and eased her back over the rail. He put his arm around her shoulder and walked her toward the foot of the bridge.

"Five minutes, Jack," said Steve solemnly.

"This is as far as I go. Get home to the people who love you. Live your life to its fullest," said Yesterman.

"Thank you. You truly are an angel," said Aimee. "Will you always be there to watch over me?"

"You will always be watched over. God is funny that way," he said.

Aimee smiled, then turned and walked away. Yesterman watched her until he could no longer see her. He then walked slowly back up the tower and through the blue mist.

***

The team stared into the pod. Steve had allowed the conversation between Jack and Aimee to be transmitted through speakers so that everyone in the room was able to hear the exchange. They were all touched by the sweetness of the moment. Steve was waiting at the pod door. When the blue haze faded, the team saw Jack holding the handrails, tears streaming down his face. Steve hurriedly opened the door as Fred rushed over to the pod.

"Are you okay? What happened? What's wrong?" Steve asked frantically.

"I miss my wife," said Jack.

15

There was no rest for the Project Yesterman team that morning. Patrick called for Max and Suzanne to return with the targeting devices, as Jack had completed the mission. Steve and Jack took a moment to pull news reports pertaining to Aimee. No reports of suicide were found. Instead, they came upon an article that profiled the opening of a new dance academy for underserved adolescents: The Donavan Connelly School of Dance Angels. One Aimee Braddock was the founder and instructor. Jack had been successful. But there was no time to celebrate. Fred whisked Jack away for another barrage of testing. The team had less than twenty-four hours to get Jack back to the past to save Holly and thus rescue Emily.

Steve had so much more planning and calculating to do for this mission. Even though he had enlisted the help of his father, he still felt rushed and unprepared. But the team worked relentlessly on pure adrenaline, coffee and an occasional granola bar. After four hours of testing, Jack finally lay down on a sofa in the study to rest. Fred analyzed the test results while Patrick honed the equipment. Max and Suzanne helped where they could. At this point it was up to Steve and his father to work through the quantum physics of getting Jack back to the time of Holly's murder. With just twelve hours before the deadline Gorski had set, Steve awakened Jack.

"Let's go for a walk," Steve said. They walked out onto the back terrace and down the steps to stroll on the expansive lawn.

"What is it that you want to talk to me about?" Jack asked, surmising that Steve wanted to speak with him privately.

"I want to make sure that you understand the implications of what it is you are about to do," said Steve. "Do you remember when I told you that if you travel back in time more than seventy-two hours, there will be a Jack Dawson of the past?"

"Yes, I remember," said Jack. "And I remember that I and the Jack Dawson of the past cannot occupy the same vibratory plane. After seventy-two hours both of us will break down and disintegrate."

"That presents some logistical problems," said Steve.

"I know, I've thought about that," said Jack.

"Have you?" asked Steve a bit skeptically. "And what have you come up with?"

"I'm going to go back as Yesterman; I'll prevent the

attack on Holly and me in the past, and then come back to the present. At least I'll see her and I'll know that she is okay and still alive in the past," he said with melancholy. "And Emily will be safe."

Steve nodded, admiring Jack's integrity, compassion and self-sacrifice; Jack was perhaps the most selfless person he had ever met. He wasn't surprised by the solution he had formulated. He knew, however, that it was the wrong solution.

"You said once that you would be willing to live those months of your life over again if you could spend them with Holly. Is that still true?" Steve asked.

"Of course it is! I would do anything to be with her," Jack said. "I just don't see how that is possible."

"Jack, you are a remarkable and gifted person," said Steve. "As Yesterman you have the ability to share your gifts. You told Aimee that her work wasn't completed, that she had a calling to fulfill. I believe the same applies to you. I believe your calling is to be Yesterman."

"I know. I feel that too. That's why I'm coming back to the present," said Jack.

"If you come back to the present, there won't be a Yesterman," said Steve. "You have to stay in the past to be Yesterman."

"What do you mean?"

"Jack, as soon as you save Holly, Yesterman will cease to be."

"Why?" Jack asked, clearly not understanding.

"When you save Holly, you and she will go home. You

will never move into the apartment above the ware-house and you will never fall into the molecular exchange beam. We will never meet and you will never take that first trip back in time," said Steve.

"So what will happen?"

"You as Yesterman will be no more the instant you save Holly. You as Jack Dawson of the past will live on. Yesterman will never come to be."

"So all we've done will mean nothing? But it's so important. There is so much more that we can do," said Jack.

"Do you truly believe that you have been called to be Yesterman? Because I do," said Steve.

"Yes, you know that I do."

"Then you have to stay in the past and you have to find me."

"How can I? Two of me can't exist together in the past."

"You have been willing to sacrifice your life to go back for Holly. Are you willing to sacrifice the life of Jack Dawson of the past?"

"What are you asking me to do, Steve?"

"Are you willing to demolecularize the Jack Dawson of the past so that Yesterman can live on with Holly?" Steve asked.

"You want me to kill myself in the past?" Jack asked incredulously.

"Yes. It's the only way that Yesterman can live on," said Steve bluntly.

Jack and Steve discussed and considered the implications. They considered the lives Jack had already saved and the many more that he could save as Yesterman. Jack struggled. He had always been willing to sacrifice his own life, but could he sacrifice his own *past* life? What would the Jack Dawson of the past think? Would he be willing to sacrifice his life to save Holly, Emily and Yesterman? *Yes, he would. Yes. I would,* concluded Jack.

"How do I do it?" Jack asked.

Steve reached into his pocket and pulled out Yesterman's polarization wristband. "Do you remember this knob?" he asked Jack, indicating the unassigned knob about which Jack had asked previously.

"Yeah, you never told me what it was for," said Jack.

"This knob activates a demolecularization field. If you face the dial toward an object and depress this knob, the object will be surrounded by that field and its molecules scattered, never to reassemble." Steve directed the face of the polarization band toward a small shrub in the yard and depressed the demolecularization knob. The familiar blue haze surrounded the shrub, and it vanished.

"So that's how I get rid of myself in the past," Jack observed. "Is it painful?"

"No, Jack, it's an instantaneous disruption of the molecular bonds. He won't feel anything," assured Steve. "For it to work, though, you must be within three feet of your target and you must be certain that the face of the polarization band is not directed at you."

"I understand, otherwise I'll vaporize myself," said Jack.

"Exactly," said Steve, nodding in affirmation.

Jack felt a wave of nausea, but he knew what he had to do. He had to ensure that Yesterman continued his calling.

Jack and Steve headed back indoors. It was time for the team to assemble and finalize the mission. They once again gathered at the round conference table in the study, and discussed the manner in which Jack would demolecularize the Jack Dawson of the past. Eventually they all agreed that it was the only solution to meet their objectives of saving Holly, Emily and Yesterman, and got down to the details of the mission. It was only two hours until Gorski's deadline.

"I remember that day like it was yesterday," Jack said. "That afternoon, before Emily's show, Holly wanted me to nap so I wouldn't complain later about the late hour. Holly went out to shop for a dress and I lay down on the sofa around 2:00 p.m. Holly came home about five. So, I figure if I get to my house by three, that will give me plenty of time to eliminate myself before Holly gets home. When she does, I'll tell her that I'm not feeling well and we'll stay home."

Suzanne and Max looked at each other. "Son, you can't do that. You *have* to go to the opening of Emily's art gallery," Max said.

"Why? If we don't go, then there will be no attack," said Jack.

"Those thugs who attacked you have to be stopped," Suzanne said. "They will keep attacking and killing. In fact, they are going to be waiting in that alley on that night whether you are there or not. Who left the gallery through that back door after you?"

"It was Emily," Max said. "She found Jack and Holly about twenty minutes after they left. No one heard the gunshots. She was just walking to her car. She will be the one that they attack."

Max looked Jack in the eyes. "Son, you have to live that night out just as it happened before," he said. "Only this time, you'll be living it as Yesterman. Those thugs have to be locked up once and for all."

Jack understood. There was no other way. Steve continued with the details of the mission. "We're going to send Jack back forty-eight hours before the attack," he said. "This will be the longest jump he has made; I want to be sure he has time to recuperate. To make sure that Jack doesn't run into himself, he will stay here with me."

"Wait a second," said Suzanne. "You're not going to know who he is. How is he going to convince you that he is from the future?"

"We've worked through that," Steve said. "Patrick has transferred to jump drives all of the data that we have accumulated regarding the molecular exchange pod, from the date that Jack will arrive in the past all the way through to today. I have also written a letter in my own hand that Jack will give to me. That too has been scanned onto one of the drives."

"So you see, all I have to do is convince Steve to open the drives," said Jack. "Nothing to it," he added sarcastically.

Steve chuckled and looked again at Suzanne. "As you can imagine, that may be easier said than done," he said. "In case you haven't noticed, I'm not the most outgoing and welcoming person. I'm quite likely to turn Jack away. And, ironically, he will be knocking on my door on April first. Go figure."

"We have worked through that as well, though," said Jack.

"Exactly," said Steve. "We have placed the targeting device behind the warehouse. I don't want him materializing inside. Though that would be quite convincing, it would also be terribly alarming. He will arrive out of sight at 9:00 a.m. Patrick, Fred and I will be working in the warehouse at that time. When I first realized that time travel was possible, I hoped that a time would come when we would transport someone back. I devised a method by which I would recognize that traveler from the future. Jack and I are the only ones who know that method. I haven't even told Patrick or Fred. Jack will convince me of who he is and from 'when' he came, and we will get him to where he needs to be to save Holly."

Steve looked around the table. He waited for questions or comments. None came. It was fifty minutes until the deadline. Steve felt that the Yesterman team was ready. It was now up to Jack.

"Whenever you're ready," Steve said to Jack.

"I'm as ready as I'll ever be," Jack replied.

"Then let's go," said Steve as he pushed back his chair and rose from the table.

The team moved from the study to the library, where the molecular exchange pod and all of its supporting equipment had been set up. Everyone stood in awkward silence until Steve spoke. "You have the plan down, right?"

"Yes, we've been over it at least a hundred times," said Jack.

Another moment of silence passed.

"This is all so surreal," Jack said. "When I see you all again, none of you will know anything of what we have all been through. Thank you all."

Jack walked to each of them in turn to say a personal goodbye before he entered the pod. He started with his father, whom he embraced.

"You have a wonderful gift, son. Use it well," said Max.

Steven Oberman, Sr. was next. "Thank you for everything you have done," said Jack.

"Good luck, be safe," said Oberman.

Then Suzanne.

"Remember, from this point on you have to protect your identity. No one can ever connect you to Yesterman or to Ken and Jennifer MacKenzie. Especially stay away from Megan Hart. Gorski is still going to be out there," cautioned Suzanne.

"I understand," said Jack.

He then addressed Steve, Patrick and Fred. "I guess

I'll see you guys in just a few minutes…just nine months ago."

"Here you go: your glasses and polarization band," said Patrick as he handed Jack the sunglasses and watch. Jack put them on. "This is the rest of your gear," as he handed Jack a large black duffle bag. Jack noticed an emblem emblazoned on the bag.

"Patrick designed it," said Fred. "We thought that Yesterman needed an emblem."

"I like it," said Jack. "Very nice touch." Patrick smiled as he shook Jack's hand. Fred took Jack's hand next. "Good luck," he said. "I'll be keeping an eye on you."

"Thanks," said Jack.

Steve approached and Jack extended his hand. But Steve ignored Jack's hand and embraced him.

"You're doing a good thing," he said. "You'll continue to do good things."

Steve released Jack and stood back. "Remember, the portal will stay open for thirty minutes if you need to abort the mission."

"Got it," said Jack. "I guess it's time."

Jack regarded the group once more, and with bag in hand entered the molecular exchange pod. Steve latched the door behind him, then took up his position at the console. He opened the communication channel.

"Are you ready?" Steve asked.

"Ready," said Jack.

"Okay, no communication on this one. You're on your own," said Steve. "Here we go. Good luck, Yesterman."

Jack gave a thumbs-up as he was enveloped in the blue electrical mist.

***

Jack emerged from the portal behind the warehouse. The jump was easier than he had expected. He would have to remember to tell Steve. He made his way to the front of the warehouse to the door. *Here goes.* He knocked on the door. There was no response. He knocked harder. The door inched open with a security chain in place. He saw half of Steve's face peering out.

"Yes?" Steve asked.

Jack stifled a laugh. He had forgotten how uptight Steve was. "Steve, I'm Jack Dawson," he said.

"I'm not interested," said Steve, and he made to close the door.

Anticipating this, Jack already had his foot wedged in place. "Schwarzschild's theory does not apply to time travel," said Jack.

Steve loosened his grip somewhat upon the door. "What is the theory?" he asked.

"Travel between universes occurs via an Einstein-Rosen bridge," replied Jack.

"How is time travel accomplished?"

"By way of refraction through vibratory planes."

Steve smiled. "Oh my God!" he exclaimed as he closed the door to release the chain. He was visibly shaking. "What is the code?"

Jack reached into his duffle bag and pulled out a ziplock bag full of jump drives. "It's all here," Jack said with a smile.

Patrick and Fred were there, and having heard the bizarre conversation, were now up close to the pair.

"What's going on?" asked Fred as Steve fumbled through the ziplock bag.

"It's a… It's…here, number one," said Steve, stumbling over his words.

He found the jump drive marked #1 and rushed over to his computer. Jack followed as Patrick and Fred eyed him warily, trailing along behind. Steve fumbled to get the drive into the USB port.

"Here, let me do it," said Patrick, taking the drive after Steve had dropped it for the second time.

Steve sat in front of the computer screen while Patrick opened the first file. It was the letter that Steve had written to himself. All three read it as Jack stood back. After Steve read the letter, he stood up and walked toward Jack, rather unsteadily. Jack, concerned that he was about to fall, rushed to support him.

"Are you okay?" Jack asked.

"From how far into the future did you come?" Steve asked.

"Nine months," said Jack.

Steve's knees buckled and Jack helped him to the sofa. "Oh my God," said Steve.

"*What* is going on?" asked Patrick.

"We don't have much time, Patrick. I need your help," said Jack.

"Who are you?" asked Fred.

"I'm Jack Dawson. I know you all from the future," said Jack. "Thanks to you, I'm Yesterman."

16

The men spent the rest of the day studying the data that Steve had sent himself from the future. Fred pored over Jack's physiologic test results while Patrick inspected all of Yesterman's protective gear and the design of the molecular exchange pod. Steve questioned Jack relentlessly as to every detail of his experience. Jack explained the circumstances of the future and the task that this team had to pull off to avert that future. It was now 7:00 p.m., exactly forty-eight hours before Emily's grand opening and art exhibit were to begin.

"This is fascinating," said Steve as he pushed away from the computer screen. "We actually did it."

The team studied, reviewed and discussed for hours. At 1:00 a.m., Steve suggested that everyone get some sleep. Fred and Patrick each took a sofa. Steve took Jack up to the apartment that in another life had been his. It looked the same except for the furniture, which consisted of a hard-backed chair in the living room and a somewhat deflated air mattress in the bedroom. But, to Jack, it was home. And he was exhausted. When Jack lay down, he fell right to sleep and slept through the night. His dreams were of Holly, and they were pleasant.

It was almost ten the next morning when Jack made it down to the warehouse. He had slept the night through. Patrick greeted him.

"How long have you guys been at it?" Jack asked.

"Since about six," said Patrick.

"You should have gotten me up."

"You needed rest," said Steve, having overheard the conversation.

"He's been up all night," said Patrick, nodding at Steve.

"Good morning," said Fred as he presented Jack with a cup of coffee. "How do you feel? Do you notice anything different from your previous travels?"

"No, I feel great. Especially after that long sleep," said Jack. He grabbed a bagel and spread some cream cheese on it. He walked over to Steve who was at his computer, looking rather disheveled.

"Why didn't I give myself more time?" Steve asked. "I feel like I'm missing something."

"It's all in there," said Jack, pointing to the computer. "You have already worked everything out."

"I don't know, something is not right, I need more time," said Steve.

"It's all there," said Jack. "What could be missing?"

"I don't know, probably nothing," said Steve. "I'm sure

I'm just anxious. I like taking time with my work. Patrick, did you check all of the equipment?"

"Yes, at least five times," said Patrick, exasperated as Steve had already asked him the same question twice before.

"We have gone over this plan time and again. We're ready," said Jack.

"Okay, I'm sure I'm just being overly cautious," said Steve. "I just wish you could at least get a look at your house before you go in."

"Believe me, I know every inch of that house. I know every minute of that day. Don't worry about that," said Jack. "Look, we're all a little uncertain, that's normal. But remember, I've done this before."

The Yesterman team worked all day and into the night. Fred ran blood tests and Patrick drove Jack by his old house in Russian Hill for a brief reconnaissance. Steve continued to learn from his own work. Something just wasn't setting right with him, however. At 10:00 p.m., he sent Patrick and Fred home and Jack to the upstairs apartment. Tomorrow was a big day. He assured the group that he would go to sleep soon. He never did.

Jack woke early that next morning. He couldn't sleep any longer. He was too excited, or maybe he was anxious about the ensuing day. This was the day for which he had been working so hard all these many months. This was the day he would resume his life with Holly. He was in the warehouse at six twenty. Steve was still at his computer with a plethora of books scattered about him.

"Hey," said Jack upon entering. He walked to the coffee pot, having been enticed by the aroma.

"Hey, Jack," said Steve, never averting his eyes from his work.

Jack poured two cups and brought one over to Steve. "Did you sleep at all?" he asked.

"I closed my eyes for a bit," said Steve. "Thank you," he said as he took the cup of coffee that Jack offered.

"It's going to be fine," said Jack.

"Oh yeah, I know," said Steve, not convincingly.

By 7:00 a.m. Patrick and Fred had arrived. The team reviewed the plan two and three times over. They talked too about what was going to happen afterwards. They discussed how Jack would continue on as Yesterman as soon as they rebuilt all of the equipment that now existed only in the future. They were proud of what they had accomplished, and of what they would accomplish. Yet Steve returned to his books and notes. Something was making him uneasy. The hours passed and it was now time for Jack to go. He was ready. It was three o'clock.

"This is it," said Steve to Jack.

"This is it," echoed Jack.

"I know that you haven't seen Holly in over nine months, but it is important that she doesn't pick up on that. You have to play it cool. You have to act just like you did the day you went to Emily's opening. It has to be as though you saw Holly last just a few hours ago."

"I understand," said Jack. "It will be difficult, but I can do it."

"Good luck and be careful," said Steve. "We'll be waiting to hear from you."

"I'll get in touch with you as soon as I can," said Jack as he shook Steve's hand. Jack then turned to Patrick. "Are you ready, Patrick?"

"Ready," said Patrick as he arose and grabbed a set of keys from the countertop.

Jack shook hands with Fred, who also wished him luck. Then he and Patrick walked out of the warehouse and got into Steve's Subaru for the drive to Russian Hill, and Jack's old house.

Jack had a familiar sensation of the surreal as he and Patrick drove in front of the house for the third time. He knew that the Jack Dawson of the present was napping on the sofa, oblivious as to what was about to transpire. Jack looked at his watch. It was 3:40. He looked too at the knob that he would soon depress, thus ending the existence of his former self. A wave of nausea again came upon him. He choked it down.

"Okay, Patrick, it's time," he said.

Patrick made the neighborhood loop one more time and parked in front of the house that backed up behind Jack's.

"Good luck," said Patrick.

Jack got out of the car and ran along the side of the

house to the rear. When he jumped the fence, he was in the back yard of his home. He made sure to conceal himself behind the shrubs lest anyone should be peering out of a window. He walked onto the back patio and tilted the potted plant concealing the spare key to his house. He inserted the key into the lock and slowly turned. The bolt slid with only the slightest click. Jack replaced the key under the pot, then opened the door to the kitchen just enough to slide through. Once in, he quietly closed the door behind him.

***

From the moment Jack and Patrick had left, Steve was once again hard at work. He knew that he was missing some important fact. He knew that something was wrong. He racked his brain for the answer, but he didn't actually know the question. He labored on. Suddenly, it hit him.

"That's it!" Steve blurted. "Oh my God, that's it!"

Fred was startled. "What's wrong?"

"How could I have missed it? How could I have been so careless?" Steve chided himself.

Steve rushed to the bookcase and pulled a book down to his desk. He thumbed through it madly. Not there. He grabbed another book and scanned its pages until he found what he needed.

"Steve, what is it?" Fred asked insistently.

"Oh my God, why did I not remember this?" Steve asked aloud.

Fred was now upon him. "What's wrong?"

Steve sank into the chair at his desk and looked up at Fred. "He's not going to disintegrate."

"Who's not going to disintegrate?"

"When Jack Dawson of the future aims the demolecularizing beam at the Jack Dawson of the present, that Jack Dawson is not going to disappear," said Steve.

"Of course he is," said Fred. "We've tested it over and over and the subjects don't reassemble."

"They don't reassemble unless there is an identical molecular match in the same vibratory plane," said Steve. "When Jack Dawson of the future demolecularizes Jack Dawson of the present, their molecules are going to merge. They have to, because they are the same."

"What does that mean for Jack, our Jack?"

"The two Jack Dawsons are going to become one being."

"What will be the result of that?' Fred asked, not sure that he wanted to know the answer.

"Their consciousness will also become one. They will have each other's memories," said Steve. "The unknown is whose consciousness will be dominant. If it is Jack Dawson of the future, there should be no problem because he has actually lived what are now memories. But if the consciousness of Jack Dawson of the present is dominant, he won't have a reference of reality for the memories he inherits from the future Jack Dawson. He has not lived those memories. His mind won't be able to process them. He'll recall fragments but they will make no sense to him."

Steve's head was hurting. He read more, and then resumed: "The theory postulates that the individual will experience a variable period of associative amnesia after the merger before the dominant consciousness surfaces."

"A fugue state," Fred said. "So he will think he has been dreaming. How long will that last?"

"Minutes, hours, days, no one knows," said Steve.

Steve looked at Fred, terror in his eyes. "We have to stop him! We have to get him back here!" he said. Steve grabbed his phone and frantically searched for Patrick's contact information. Just as he was about to place the call, Patrick walked through the door wearing a grin of success.

"He made it, no problems," he said proudly.

***

Jack eased through the kitchen and stood at the passageway leading into the den. He saw the back of the sofa upon which he knew the present Jack Dawson to be sleeping. He heard the sound of his slow and rhythmic breathing. Jack circled the sofa, careful to direct the dial of the watch away from himself. He froze for a moment when he saw himself asleep, the most surreal experience yet. In that moment of hesitation, the present Jack Dawson opened his eyes with a start. Jack Dawson of the future quickly depressed the demolecularizing knob as the other Jack grabbed his arm and pulled him forward. The blue haze engulfed them both. Jack felt the spinning vortex to which he had become accustomed. It was much stronger this time. He felt as though his body was being injected by a million needles. *I've just killed us both* he thought as his world went dark.

Jack Dawson's dreams came in bursts. They consisted of random images of people, places and things both recognizable and unrecognizable. They came in crazy sequences with no cohesion. He awoke for a moment and found his body to be drenched with sweat and contorted upon the sofa. He ached mightily. He straightened himself and fell back to a peaceful sleep.

Holly arrived back home around five, loaded with bags from her shopping excursion. She had run out to pick up a "little something" to wear to Emily's grand opening. She now had three dresses and four pairs of shoes from which to choose.

"Jack, I'm home," she called out.

There was no response. She walked through the living room, saw that the sofa was unoccupied and headed upstairs.

"Jack?" she called again as she entered their bedroom and dropped her bags upon the bed.

"Hey baby," said Jack as he emerged from the bathroom, tying his necktie. "Looks like you tore it up at the shops," he laughed as he noted Holly's purchases.

"Hi, honey," Holly said as she received his embrace and kiss. "Did you rest well?"

"Yeah, I did. I had some crazy dreams though," he said.

"Are you still worried that Emily's open house isn't going to be successful?" Holly asked.

"I don't know. I just have this feeling that something bad is going to happen," said Jack. "I'm sure that I'm just nervous for her."

"I can assure you that she has everything under control," said Holly confidently. "You know her; it's going to be great!"

"Yeah, you're right," conceded Jack.

Holly gave Jack a kiss on the cheek as she slid past him and into the master bathroom. "I'm going to get ready," she said. "How about you make me a Grey Goose and tonic to get our celebration started?"

"You got it, my love," said Jack, and he headed downstairs.

The night was a complete success for Emily. Max and Sarah had left a couple of hours before and all that remained were Emily, Jack, Holly, and a few gallery workers. Jack and Holly were saying their goodbyes to Emily.

"You did great! I'm so happy for you," said Holly as she embraced Emily.

"Thank you. And thanks for tearing that big nerd

away from work to be here," said Emily, nodding toward Jack.

"Believe me, he wouldn't have missed it. He has been so nervous that something was going to go wrong tonight. He has been obsessing over it," said Holly.

"Really! No doubts, huh? You big liar," said Emily to Jack, remembering his earlier comment.

Holly released Emily and turned to her husband. "So much for your premonitions," Holly joked. She entwined her arm in Jack's.

"Come on, lover boy, let's go home," she said.

Jack gave Emily a kiss on the cheek. "Bye, I'll call you tomorrow," he said.

Jack and Holly made their way to the rear of the gallery, out the back door and into the alley. It was a cold night and Holly huddled next to her husband as they walked toward the main street fronting the gallery. Halfway down, three figures emerged from the shadows some distance ahead of them. Knowing that the door to the gallery had locked behind him, Jack pressed forward. Holly noticed them too.

"Jack, what…?"

"Just keep walking, baby," he instructed.

The men spread out as they walked toward Jack and Holly, effectively blocking the alley. It wasn't until the three were upon them that Jack realized they were wearing ski masks. The apparent leader addressed them.

"Well looky what we got here. We got us a couple

of high-class artsy-fartsies. And look at this pretty little thing," said the lead thug referring to Holly.

He then pulled a handgun and pointed it at Jack's head. One of his accomplices pulled a knife and rounded behind Holly. She froze as he held the blade to her neck.

"Look man, we don't want any trouble," said Jack. "Here, take my wallet, there's plenty of cash in it." Jack took his wallet from his back pants pocket and tossed it at the feet of the gunman. "And here, my watch; take my watch. It's a Rolex." Jack unclasped the watch and tossed it as well. The gunman picked it up to admire it.

"That's real nice of ya," he said. "Looky here boys; we got us one of them charitable snobs."

The two other thugs laughed.

"That's all that we have, now let us go on our way," implored Jack.

As the gunman put the watch and wallet in his jacket pocket, he eyed Holly. "Oh no, you got one more thing that I want," said the gunman.

Jack lunged toward the gunman, who then fired the weapon. Jack heard Holly's scream as the crack from the gun faded. He grew lightheaded as his knees buckled and he fell to the ground. The pain he felt was intense. He clutched his chest, unable to breathe. As he lay on his side, he saw Holly being dragged further down the alley. Suddenly, his breath came to him, the wind having been knocked out of him by the impact of the bullet into his etartenepon protected chest. With lightning speed he was upon Holly's abductor. The thug moved to slash

Holly. Jack tackled him and in doing so Holly was knocked back and fell, her head striking a water valve that was protruding from the wall of the building next door to the gallery. She lay unconscious upon the dirty street.

As soon as Jack disarmed the thug, a second thug was upon him, driving a knife into Jack's back. The blade fractured upon hitting the etartenepon bodysuit that Jack wore beneath his clothing. As the second thug stood dumbfounded, Jack reared back his head and caught the man between the eyes, knocking him out cold. As the first thug made to rise, Jack caught him with an uppercut just beneath the right-side rib cage and into the liver. It took a moment before the intense pain hit, dropping the thug to the ground and incapacitating him.

"You can stop right there," said the gunman.

Jack turned slowly to see that the man had taken off his ski mask, revealing himself, shaved head and all. "I'm going to enjoy watching you die," said the skinhead through a sardonic grin.

He fired his weapon, which was aimed squarely at Jack's head. Jack saw the flash from the barrel, followed by the bullet coursing on its trajectory toward him in slow motion. He easily side-stepped the projectile and casually made his way to the skinhead who appeared to be frozen in time, gun in hand. Jack disarmed the man and bound his hands and feet with cable ties that he retrieved from the inner coat pocket of his suit jacket. Suddenly all motion was back to normal speed. Jack quickly ran over to the other two men and bound their wrists to a nearby drainpipe. Jack then went over to Holly, who was starting to rouse. He pulled out a handkerchief and dabbed the blood from her head.

"Hey punk," shouted the skinhead. "You think I'm done with you? You think they're gonna keep me locked up? No way, man, I'm coming back for you. And your little bitch."

Jack walked over to the skinhead and reached into his jacket pocket to retrieve his wallet and watch. He put the wallet in his back pant pocket and the watch upon his wrist.

"Who are you, anyway?" the skinhead asked.

Jack did not respond. Instead, he made his way back toward Holly.

"Hey punk, I'm talking to you! I asked you who you are!"

Jack looked at the other thugs and saw that they too were starting to rouse. He walked over to the skinhead, who smirked, "Yeah, you best come when I call you, punk."

Jack looked down and considered the man for a moment. He then pulled up his sleeve and directed the face of his watch toward the man.

"I'm Yesterman," said Jack.

He depressed a knob and a blue mist surrounded the skinhead. In a blink he was gone, leaving only a puddle of water in his place. "Not such a tough guy now, are you?" said Jack softly as he turned from the vacant space.

Jack walked over to Holly. "Baby, wake up," he said.

Holly looked up at her husband. "What happened?"

"Nothing, baby, everything is okay."

"My head hurts."

"I know, baby," said Jack. "Can you stand?"

"I think so," she said.

Jack helped Holly to her feet and swept her into his arms. He held her tightly. It seemed a lifetime since he had felt her against him, and he never wanted to let her go. After a few moments, Jack finally relaxed his grip and looked into Holly's eyes.

"I missed you so much," he said with tears welling in his eyes.

"What are you talking about? Are you okay?" Holly asked.

"I'm great. I love you, baby."

"I love you too," said Holly as she wiped a tear from Jack's cheek.

"Let's go home," said Jack.

Holly grabbed Jack's arm and rested her head upon his shoulder as they walked. Jack pulled his cell phone from his pocket and called 911.

"Nine-one-one; what's your emergency?" said the operator.

"There is a mugging in progress in the alley next to Arte del Tiempo," said Jack.

"What is your name, sir?" the operator asked.

Jack disconnected the call. Holly noticed something

different about Jack as she caressed his arm. "Have you been working out?" she asked.

"You have no idea," said Jack.

They reached the main road and turned right to stroll down the sidewalk toward their car. Jack pulled Holly close to him, shielding her against the cool air. A fog was settling upon the city, just starting to obscure the moon and stars above. Jack had the thought that the sky couldn't decide whether it wanted to rain or snow. He felt an unsettling sense of familiarity; a sense of déjà vu that he couldn't quite place. Jack pushed the feeling away and said a silent prayer of thanks as he took his wife home to the yellow house in Russian Hill.

EPILOGUE

The eastbound traffic of the interstate was at a dead stop. There had been no movement for over twenty minutes. The westbound lane, however, was moving freely. In that lane an eighteen-wheeler sped under the overpass, swerving wildly with its trailer teetering behind.

Yesterman emerged from behind the support pillar of the overpass just as the truck went by, running at breakneck speed. The truck had crossed over the fourth lane of the westbound side and was heading into the median. Yesterman jumped upon the running board of the truck on the driver's side and pried the door open. The driver was slumped over onto the passenger side. Yesterman wedged himself into the cab and engaged the brakes. The truck jackknifed and skidded to a halt a mere five feet from the driver-side door of a Mazda 6 standing idle in the eastbound lane.

Yesterman saw a small cooler overturned in the truck's passenger seat with its contents scattered upon the floorboard. He reached down and retrieved a small bottle of milk. He was able to rouse the driver enough to have him sip some of it.

"What happened?" asked the driver groggily.

"Your glucose level is too low," said Jack. "Here, take another sip."

"Can I help?" asked a young woman, running up to the window. "I'm a nurse."

"Yes, please," said Yesterman. "This man is diabetic. He's had an insulin reaction. Call 911."

Yesterman handed the young woman the milk bottle and jumped down from the cab. After he helped her up into the cab, he walked over to the Mazda. He saw a young man in the driver's seat, obviously shaken. Yesterman tapped on the window, startling the young man, who rolled down the window.

"Are you okay?" asked Yesterman.

"Yeah, yeah I'm fine," said the young man tremulously. "I thought I was going to die. I froze, I couldn't move."

"It's okay, you're going to be fine."

"You saved my life, thank you," said the young man. "Man, I really thought I was going to die."

"Not today, Donavan, you've got many more years ahead of you." Yesterman then turned and began to walk away.

"Hey, how do you know my name?" Donavan asked. "Who are you?"

Yesterman turned and faced Donavan. "I'm Yesterman. Now you get home to Aimee, she loves you very much. Be good to that girl. She is a treasure," he said. With that, Yesterman turned and bolted away.

Megan Hart had witnessed the whole event from her

car, stuck in traffic two cars behind the car of Donavan Connelly. She could have sworn that she saw a blue flash as the mysterious man rounded the pillar of the over-pass, and vanished.

The End

* 9 7 8 0 9 9 6 3 9 6 6 2 2 *